The Submarine Privateer,

A TALE OF

THE GREAT BOER WAR,

AND

The Land of Mystery,

A STORY OF

INDIAN MARVELS.

BOTH WRITTEN BY

THOMAS LE BRETON.

ILLUSTRATED BY E. L. TODÉ.

LONDON :

HARKAWAY HOUSE, 6, WEST HARDING STREET, FETTER LANE,
FLEET STREET, E.C., AND ALL BOOKSELLERS.

"THE BOER FELL BELOW, SHOT THROUGH THE HEAD."

No. 1.

The Submarine Privateer.

CHAPTER I.

In the early portion of 1901, the newspapers were full of conjectures concerning the strange disappearance of British vessels. Quite a number, both of steamers and sailing-vessels, had vanished in a manner that could not be accounted for.

Some people wrote to the editors, suggesting that some great marine animal had caused this wholesale destruction, some that a strangely virulent disease had destroyed the crews; some few thought that the friends of the Boers had placed explosives on board which had sunk the ill-fated vessels.

At Lloyds', every day some other vessels or vessel were posted as overdue, and this from all parts, but chiefly from vessels trading in the Atlantic, and it was felt that some means must be taken by the Government to set the nation at rest. But the British Government, with their hands full with the Boer War in South Africa, made no sign, and many were the mourners in Britain, as friends and relatives did not arrive at port.

The ss. "Aurora" was one of the missing steamers, and this ill-fated vessel had sailed from Monte Video for England all well.

On board were Professor Grant and his two daughters, Marjory and Beth; and among others, Gilbert Romer, barrister at law, and Bob, his young nephew, were plunged in deep grief as day by day passed without news.

*   *   *   *

Gilbert Romer was seated in his rooms in the Inner Temple with an open map before him.

He was deep in some gloomy thoughts, so that he did not hear the knock at his outer door until it had been repeated three or four times, when he rose with a sigh and opened the door.

The caller was a broad-shouldered, bright-looking lad of about fifteen years of age; some twelve years younger than Gilbert himself.

"Any news, uncle?" he asked.

"No, Bob," was the reply; "nothing at all."

"Then I have something to tell you," said Bob, excitedly, opening a newspaper which he held in his hands. "Look here, uncle," and he read the following extract from the *Daily Express*:

"The captain of the ss. 'Valentia,' which arrived at Liverpool on Saturday last, reports that in mid-ocean, on his way to Monte Video, his steamer was boarded by a white pigeon that bore a scrap of paper, on which was written in a childish hand 'Follow us.' The secret of this strange message has yet to be found, but it is conjectured that some vessel has sunk, and that the unfortunate crew has taken to the boats. Captain Wallis thinks that it may have something to do with the disappearance of the ss. 'Aurora,' which is now some weeks overdue, and which has not been heard of in any way. If that is so, it is probably too late to send help. The 'Aurora' was last spoken not 200 miles from where the pigeon was found. Captain Wallis was on his way to Monte Video then, and as soon as he returned to England he reported the finding of the bird. It seems a pity that the captain of the ss. ' Valentia' did not at once report the find at Monte Video, or, if he did so, that the British Consul did not institute a search. However, the whole affair is wrapt in mystery, and the truth will probably never be arrived at."

"There," said Bob, excitedly; "that's Beth's pigeon, I am sure of it. We must go to Liverpool at once, uncle, and see the piece of paper."

"We will go, Bob," replied Gilbert Romer, taking the time-table from his desk, "but I am afraid it will be a useless journey. We shall follow them sure enough one day, when our time comes, for I have not the slightest hope that they are alive."

Gilbert Romer had been engaged for some time to Marjory Grant, and her father had promised that on their return to England the marriage should take place.

'Beth, who was two years Bob's junior, it was understood, was to grow up on purpose to make Bob the wife that he particularly desired.

Of course, such an engagement was informal and unrecognised, but nevertheless Bob was attached with all a boy's ardour to his little sweetheart, and he was as deeply concerned about the missing " Aurora" as his uncle.

For days past they had searched the papers; they had inquired at Lloyds' and of the owners; they had interviewed old mariners who knew the secrets of the seas, and day by day hope had grown fainter, until at last Gilbert had settled down to a deep despair.

Bob's younger and more sanguine nature had not altogether parted with hope yet, and to him this message from the deep bore all manner of possibilities.

It was a little afterwards that the two were hurrying to Liverpool by express train, and before five o'clock that same afternoon they were on board the " Valentia " in the Prince's Dock, Liverpool, where the great steamer was lying while discharging her cargo.

The chief officer was on board tallying at the main hatch, and he referred them to the steward, who, when he heard of their errand, took them into the cabin and showed them the white pigeon in a wicker cage.

"That's 'Beth's pigeon," cried Bob, excitedly. "Where is the writing?"

Gilbert looked sadly at the pretty bird, which was pluming itself unconcernedly.

Were those whom it had left, lying deep down in their last sleep?

To him it seemed that the reason that the bird had escaped was that its mistress desired to save its life when she, and those with her, were in their last peril.

"That's 'Beth's writing; look, uncle," cried Bob. as he showed the smudged words, which had been written in pencil on a tiny slip of paper, " Follow us."

"Uncle, I do not mean to give up hope of finding them even if you do. 'Beth has asked us to follow them, and I mean to search even if I have to work my way out to Monte Video as a ship's boy."

"Do not be too confident, Bob," said his uncle, sadly. "It is our duty to search, and in that I shall join you, though I fear it is of no use."

They were returning to London that same night.

Bob, with a pile of papers beside him, for he was careful to let no item of news pass without considering it, looked up at his uncle with a puzzled expression.

"Do you see what those Boers are up to?" he asked.

"What's that, Bob? I am afraid I have too much to think of just now to follow the war."

"Well, this paper says that the *Eclair*, of Paris, published on Aug. 13th, has interviewed Senator Pauliat, President of the Boer Independence Committee, who says the probable effect of Lord Kitchener's proclamation will be that the Boers will soon authorise privateering, and that the British merchant fleet will be annihilated in a few months. The *Eclair* thinks that no Power will object."

"That's all bounce, my boy. If a privateer sailed from any port, our cruisers would know of it at once, and she would have no chance."

"But, uncle, supposing they got hold of one of those submarines? All the countries hate us, and would keep their doings dark. You know that the loss of British vessels of late has been three times the average loss for this time of year?"

"We do not know what bad weather some of the missing vessels may have met."

"Oh, yes, we do, uncle. That is already reported, and there has been nothing to account for these disasters. All of the papers are noticing these heavy losses, and are asking what can be the cause. I know the cause," cried the boy excitedly, springing to his feet. "The Boers have got a submarine, and, what is more, they have destroyed the 'Aurora.'"

"Bob! Bob! Can it be possible?"

And Gilbert Romer became almost as excited as his nephew.

"It is possible. Think it out, uncle, and you will see it is. What is more, the Boers are not savages. They would rescue those on board before sinking the ship. They have probably made the Grants prisoners, and have got them in some unknown place, and that is why 'Beth sent the message, 'Follow us.'"

"The first thing to-morrow morning I shall go and see the Admiralty," said Gilbert, with determination. "The more I think of it, the more I can see how reasonable your conjecture is."

And, still talking the matter over, the two returned to London.

CHAPTER II.

WITHOUT waiting a moment longer than was absolutely necessary, Gilbert Romer called at the Admiralty.

He had some difficulty in seeing one of the heads of the departments, and to him Gilbert stated his case, quoting a number of paragraphs from certain foreign papers to show that the Boers were encouraging privateering.

"My dear sir," said the Secretary, courteously, "it is quite excusable for any member of the outside public to imagine such things as you have done, but let me assure you that it would be absolutely impossible for any vessel, submarine or otherwise, to leave a foreign port without our knowing anything of it here. Why, my dear sir," he added, "every foreign government knows that the British Admiralty have eyes everywhere, and an arm that reaches to the uttermost seas."

"But how do you account for this sudden increase of missing vessels amongst our shipping?"

"Chance, my dear sir, merely chance. The laws of average will soon put that right. We have had a bad three months; by and bye we shall have a very light three months to make up for it."

In vain Gilbert argued.

The Secretary was always polite, but absolutely firm.

Gilbert endeavoured to see other officials at the Admiralty, but it was useless.

He interviewed his member of Parliament, and persuaded him after some trouble—for he was a Pro-Boer and believed that the Boers could do no harm—to ask a question in the House; but in the Commons the idea was merely laughed at, in spite of the fact that Mr. Tommy Bowles took up the matter—probably for the sake of girding at the Government.

He told them some of the feats that the French and American submarines had already attempted, which proved that the Boer submarine was not only a possibility, but a probability.

However, nothing came of all this.

In addition to seeing the Admiralty officials and his member of Parliament, the young barrister (for Gilbert had been called to the Bar the year before) wrote to all the leading newspapers of the Kingdom; but although in one or two cases the editors admitted that a submarine boat belonging to an enemy could do British shipping an enormous amount of harm, still one and all maintained that such a vessel could never escape the vigilance of the British Government, and that it was only a false hope for the safety of the "Aurora's" passengers that was leading Mr. Romer astray.

In some papers a good deal of correspondence ensued, and one correspondent even went so far as to propose floating a limited company which would build a submarine boat that should act against any enemy's vessel that existed.

Gilbert called upon this man in the hope that a few patriotic Britishers would combine to make some effort to solve the mystery; but when he found that the man merely wished to act as secretary with a substantial salary, and to use him for getting subscriptions together, he had nothing more to do with the scheme.

He and Bob had given way to despair, when one day, nearly a fortnight after his visit to the Admiralty, he received a call from Sir Peter Patterson, a well-known South African millionaire.

He was a man nearer sixty than fifty years of age, with grizzled hair, but with a well-knit and sturdy frame, that years of adventure on the veldt had toughened.

"I have called with reference to your correspondence in the *Times*," he said to Gilbert as soon as he had made matters known. "I suppose that you have not been able to persuade the Government to move in the matter?"

"No! No one seems to believe in what we suggest," answered Gilbert, while Bob broke in hotly with, "They're a lot of fools."

Sir Peter smiled at the boy's vehemence.

"Most men who are in well-paid positions which they have not won by their own merit *are* fools, my boy," he said. "Only those who have won their way by their wits have enough sense to run an Empire properly. Fortunately, every Government is pretty bad, or ours would not have a look in. But now," he added, turning to Gilbert, "your idea is, I gather, to build a submarine and search for the one that

you think the Boers are now running."

"Yes, Sir Peter, that is so," answered Gilbert, "but I am as far off my object as ever. I have very little money myself, and to build such a submarine as I want they tell me will cost close on £400,000."

"Four hundred thousand pounds," mused the millionaire; "and I am worth—well, I am worth a lot more than that, Mr. Romer."

Bob looked up keenly.

He was quite prepared for the offer which was coming.

"You see, Mr. Romer," continued Sir Peter, "I have lived among the Boers, and I know their slim ways. To run a submarine, and damage their enemy with next to no risk to themselves is just what would delight these gentlemen. I suppose you have not heard, as the Admiralty keep matters so dark, that H.M. sloop 'Boadicea' is supposed to be lost with all hands? They cannot account for it, but I think that your theory would explain matters quite well. Anyhow, if you will come with me, we will go down to Yarrow's, the torpedo-boat builders, who are pretty smart people for getting a job through in a hurry, and see what they can do for us. I have been recommended there."

"And you will buy a submarine?" gasped Gilbert, almost too surprised for words.

"That is my intention," answered the millionaire. "If I like my pleasure yacht to go under the sea instead of over it, like those of my friends, who is to gainsay me?"

"And will she be armed?" asked Bob, eagerly.

"Yes, my lad, she shall have enough deadly weapons aboard to please even the British schoolboy. If we should happen to meet a Boer submarine, she won't surrender to us if we merely float out a Union Jack. There is only one thing will make a Boer agree with you. You must just show him that if he does not give in he will go to Kingdom Come. Once he sees that you mean business, he will be as agreeable a man, except for his dirt, as you will come across. You can come with us, my boy. My carriage is outside."

It seemed like a dream, when, a few minutes after, they were rattling through the town towards the East End, where on the river Messrs. Yarrow and Co. have their shipbuilding yards.

After half-an-hour's talk with the manager there, he showed them drawings for a submarine vessel, which he said would be better than the best that had been built by any nation.

"It is our own design, Sir Peter," he said, "and it has a number of improvements that we do not care to give away to the general public. You see this audiphone?" and he pointed to an instrument like a compass.

Bob looked closely into it, eager to find its secret.

"It is not in working order," said the manager, "but it will go into the submarine. It records all sound within a mile, the volume being noted on the scale, in addition to which the index will point in the direction from which the sound comes. Thus, if another vessel is near, the sound of it will be indicated at once. Here is another patent," and the manager, after one or two mysterious movements with an instrument hanging near the window, darkened the room. Then, a moment after, a brilliant light shot out from the instrument, and a picture was shown in magic-lantern fashion on a screen close by.

Men were seen at work on a vessel, their every movement distinct.

"Magic lantern with a reflector?" asked Bob, who generally knew a bit about everything

"Not exactly," said the manager, "but something like it. These men are at work the other side of a wall. We use a species of X-rays which enable us to direct the rays of light through any solid body, in much the same way as the present X-rays are used."

"But what's the use of that to us?" asked Sir Peter.

"In this way," said the manager. "You are aware that the waves of the sea, the waves of sound, and the waves of light, all possess the same motion. We have taken advantage of that, and this instrument will take a photograph of things moving nearly a quarter of a mile away through the water intervening."

"Marvellous!" said Gilbert. "Then, of course, if it will do this, the secret of submarine navigation is found. I know that the great difficulty hitherto has been that it was impossible for a submarine vessel to see ahead. Now, we shall know exactly what is in front or beside us. Is that not so?"

"It is so," answered Messrs. Yarrow's representative. "And equipped as your vessel will be, you will find that she will be more than a match for anything afloat, either above or beneath the sea. The Admiralty might possess these improvements of ours were they not so old-fashioned in their ideas. As it is, you will be the first to use them."

Sir Peter, before he left, had signed a contract for the vessel, which would be delivered within six weeks; a huge sum for one person to pay, nearer half a million of money than four hundred thousand.

"Too short a time," the manager had said, but the millionaire offered to make it worth his while to work night and day with all the best men available.

For six weeks Sir Peter and Gilbert were continually at the sheds where the submarine was being built in an enclosure safe from prying eyes.

Bob, too, came down whenever he could get away from school.

Quickly the monster grew, until the day of launching was settled, and the captain and the crew engaged.

Built all of aluminium, and propelled by petrol, the great vessel was capable of going for 13,000 miles at half-speed without renewing the fuel supply.

She was 217 feet in length, and in diameter 24 feet 7 inches, whilst her conning-tower was 36 inches in diameter, and was protected by 6 inches of nickel rolled armour.

She carried eighteen torpedoes, six of which were Brennans—these being controlled from the vessel—besides several rapid-firing guns.

The extraordinary boat had two

hulls, one inside the other, the outsides joined by T-shaped irons, which rendered it very strong.

Owing to this cellular arrangement, it was capable of resisting like a block—as if it were solid.

Its sides would never yield, as it cohered spontaneously, and not by the closeness of its rivets, and the homogenity of its construction, due to the perfect and matchless union of the materials, would enable the submarine to hold her own in the stormiest ocean. The two hulls were composed of aluminium plates whose density was from seven to eight—that of water—the first two being two inches thick, weighing three hundred tons; the second weighing fifty-eight tons; the engines, with electric light appliances, with other accessories and apparatus, weighing some ninety tons.

All this, with fearful and powerful steel rams, made the submarine indeed an aquatic monster.

Diving dresses, with air reservoirs, by means of which a number of men could remain under water detached from all assistance for from three to four hours, were provided, and, in addition to other necessaries, stores and provisions were taken on board to last for six months.

It was on an early spring morning that the launch took place, just at the time of sunrise.

The ordinary workers had not yet left their homes, and the few who were necessary for the work in hand were gathered round the shed wherein lay the great vessel that was soon to know the secrets of the under seas.

On the river some half-dozen barges were floating quietly along, with the lightermen pulling at the great sweeps that guided them on the tide.

The manager of Messrs. Yarrow's was looking around to see that everything was in order for his final work.

"We are ready, Sir Peter," he said at last, "if you are."

"Quite ready," answered the millionaire; and, shaking hands with the manager, he, with Gilbert and Bob, went on board and screwed down the hatch by which they reached the hold.

"Father would not have let me come, Uncle Gil, had you not promised to take care of me," said Bob, as he looked round, with pleasure beaming in every line of his face.

"Well, we talked him over all right, Bob, but if your mother had been alive, I am afraid you would not be now one of the crew of the 'Nautilus.'"

"We are moving," interrupted Sir Peter. "Now for the first plunge."

And surely enough, the submarine, slowly at first, began to gather speed, and, to the surprise of the few onlookers, who had not before seen her, she shot into the river, as unshiplike a looking craft as they had ever seen.

There was a swirl of waters, a few heavy waves, and then the hull of the vessel disappeared in the sweeping current, leaving only the conning-tower showing above the turbid stream.

CHAPTER III.

As soon as the submarine ship "Nautilus" started on her voyage down the Thames, Bob had time to look around.

The state-cabin was a large, handsome room, fitted with blue and silver, the door-handles, pillars, and all metal-work being silver-plated.

Leading from the state-room were four berths, one for Captain Deane,

and one each for Sir Peter, Gilbert, and Bob.

These were all fitted up as in a high-class yacht, and Bob looked at his snug little room with great pride.

Outside the cabin-door was the steward's pantry, and the lad gazed at the appetising stores there with hungry eyes.

Beyond this, again, and shut off by a door, was the cook's galley, where Jake, the cook, was already preparing breakfast.

A water-tight door led into the centre of the ship, where the great engines were, and beyond this again was the forecastle, in which the men had their berths, the engineers having a small room just off the engine-room.

No A.B.'s were carried, the crew being practically all engineers.

Mr. Buchan, the chief engineer, was busily engaged trying the engines, when Sir Peter and his friends entered.

"Do they work well?" the millionaire asked.

"Perfectly, Sir Peter," was the reply. "One would think that they had been running for a month, they go so easily. There is no chance of a hot bearing here, and, thank goodness, we have no water-tubes to burst. This petrol is a wonderful invention, sir."

"How many knots do you think we can get out of her under water?" Sir Peter asked of Captain Deane.

"We will try that, Sir Peter, when we get into blue water," replied the skipper. "We must go carefully here. There is too much shipping about, and not much water for us to keep out of sight in. Then, too, it is not easy to follow the Channel unless we rise now and again."

"Very well, captain. Then, as soon as we get down Channel we'll test her. Where are the air reservoirs?"

The captain pointed to a row of cylinders that apparently went all round the vessel.

"We have enough here to last us, with care, for one hundred and twenty hours, filtering with chemicals, and using every care."

"Well, we are not likely to remain five days under water," said Sir Peter, "so that we ought to have enough and to spare. Who is responsible for keeping them charged?"

"I am, Sir Peter," Mr. Buchan answered, "and you may be sure that every time we go to the surface I shall see that the storage-pumps are used. There is no knowing what difficulties we may get into, and

there is nothing like being on the safe side."

"A careful man that, captain," said Sir Peter, after they had left the engine-room.

"You want a careful man, Sir Peter," replied the shipmaster, "and in modern vessels the engineer shares quite half the responsibility with the captain. Buchan is a *very* careful man, and, as you have noticed, he is a Scotchman, and they always make the best engineers."

"Are you ready for breakfast, sir?" the steward asked, as he stood at the door.

Captain Deane looked at Sir Peter inquiringly, and Sir Peter caught Bob's eye.

"I can see one of us is quite ready for breakfast," said the millionaire, laughing. "Let's have it, captain, for my friend Bob looks quite appealing in his hunger."

"Men who have to fight must eat well," said Bob, grandiloquently, at which the others laughed; and Bob soon showed that if he could fight as well as he could eat, there was the making of one of the bravest soldiers in the world in him.

The captain did not sit down with them, but betook himself to the conning-tower, the navigation of the river being somewhat difficult.

About mid-day the vessel was off the Nore.

A fresh breeze and a merry sea caused her to roll a bit when she was near the surface; and Bob was beginning to look a bit grave, while Sir Peter disappeared into his cabin.

"You will be all right in a little time," said Captain Deane, as he came into the cabin for a few moments. "We will go under soon, and then we shall be as still as a penny steamer running above bridges."

"Would you like to come into the conning-tower for a little while, Master Bob?" the captain said, a little later; and Bob, curious to see all that there was to be seen, went and looked through the thick glass, which under water had to stand such enormous pressure.

Just ahead was a large steamer coming towards them, and the captain squeezed himself up quickly, forcing Bob below.

Then came a perceptible movement, and a louder rushing of waters; darkness in the conning-tower for two or three minutes, after which tne dull light again broke through, and the captain made way for Bob.

"We dived under her," said the skipper. "I wanted to test our capabilities. We have a very handy vessel here, young sir, and Sir Peter ought to be very proud of her. She will very nearly turn in her own length, and work down ten feet in forty yards, or sink as straight as a stone."

The vessel was now making for the North Foreland, preparatory to entering the Channel, and Gilbert fetched Bob to show him the armament.

Great fish-torpedoes, that lay in cradles, ready to be pushed into the tube; and quick-firing guns, that would spit out shells at the rate of ten per minute; but what took the boy's fancy most was a pretty little Mauser rifle, before which he stood admiringly.

"That would make the Boers run," he said.

"That is about your size, eh, Bob?" said Sir Peter, coming up behind the lad.

"It is a real beauty!" he cried.

"You may look at it," observed Sir Peter; and Bob eagerly grasped the weapon and examined it, and saw, to his delight, a plate let into the butt, on which were engraved the words, "Bob Romer."

"That is your own, Bob," said the millionaire, "and as soon as we get into quiet waters we are all going to have some rifle and gun practice. There is no knowing when we may be called upon to use our weapons."

Bob was charmed with the gift, and spent the next hour or so in marching about the cabin and worrying Gilbert who was a lieutenant in the Inns of Court Volunteers, to put him through his drill.

In the afternoon they rose to the surface of the water, being now in the open Channel, and lying so low in the water that they were hardly observed by passing vessels.

A light rail was rigged round the after-part of the vessel, which could be unshipped again in less than two minutes.

On the promenade which this enclosed, Sir Peter and his friends walked up and down, the sea just now being very smooth, and the keen air reviving them.

A considerable way ahead a huge, ugly mass of iron could be seen steaming slowly towards them.

"That's a very ugly liner, Captain Deane," Sir Peter said.

The skipper, who was looking at her, answered:

"French man-o'-war, Sir Peter. That's 'La Gloire,' one of the biggest ships the Frenchmen have; but she is very clumsy, and cannot do more than thirteen knots."

"What can we get out of the 'Nautilus,' captain?" Gilbert asked.

"Twenty-four knots on the surface, eight knots below," was the reply.

"You have tested her, then?" asked Sir Peter.

"Yes, Sir Peter, and she's a knot better than the guarantee."

"Cannot we give the Frenchman a little surprise?" Bob queried. "I should like to frighten them," he added, with a grin.

Sir Peter smiled, and turned to Captain Deane.

"We might try a little manœuvre to see how we could attack a big vessel, captain."

Captain Deane nodded.

"I am quite ready, sir. Shall we go within a hundred yards and hail her, and then make a dive?"

"Certainly," was the answer. "And you might try that dummy torpedo."

"It will be rather awkward taking it up afterwards, Sir Peter, if we frighten them. They may turn nasty."

"We shall not want it again. You can leave it after you have fired it."

Bob stole down to the torpedo-room, where one of the men, who had been in the navy, and knew how to fire these weapons, was put in charge.

Old Davy Seaforth grinned as he saw the boy busy with a pot of white paint and a brush, with which he was painting some words on the torpedo.

"This is to be a present for Froggy," he said, and the old man grinned again.

"Don't you wish it was loaded, Davy?" Bob asked, while he kept on with his work.

"Well, I can't say as I do, sir," said the old salt. "When I was a young man I was always hoping we would have a brush with the French; but when I came to know them better, they aren't a bad sort, and if we don't rub them up the wrong way they are civil enough to us."

"But they are such braggers," Davy."

"Well, so they are sir," was the reply, "and no doubt what you are doing now will cure them of a little of that. There's been no holding them in since they had those submarines of theirs, although they might have known by this time that if they had got a good submarine, Great Britain was sure to have a better."

The "Nautilus" approached "La Gloire" at full speed until within a couple of hundred yards.

Then Captain Deane opened the lid of the conning-tower, and hailed the Frenchman.

The reply came back:

"Who are you?"

Instead of replying, Captain Deane slammed down the hatch, and with a rapid turn of the handle screwed it tight.

The speaking-tube communicating with the engine-room was next quickly in use, and, to the Frenchmen's horror, the submarine dived and approached her.

Soon it stopped, and Sir Peter, using the X-ray machine for the first time, saw depicted on the canvas the keel of the man-of-war.

Suddenly, with a hiss, the dummy torpedo was sent off, and on the screen it could be seen swiftly approaching the hull of "La Gloire," just amidships.

It struck, rebounded, and rose to the surface.

The dull boom of artillery sounded overhead.

The Frenchmen were evidently firing into the water in the hope of hitting them; and so, putting on full speed, Captain Deane sent his vessel under the French man-o-war, and only came to the surface again a mile distant.

"They have sent a boat to pick up our torpedo, Sir Peter," he said.

Bob was dancing with delight.

"It will do them a great deal of good this time," he cried.

"Why, what have you done to it, Bob?" Sir Peter asked.

"I painted on it these words," the boy replied: "*Under the sea and on the sea Britannia rules!*"

"And she always will rule," said Sir Peter. "But we had better not stop for them. Let's get along down Channel, captain."

And so the "Nautilus" proceeded on her voyage.

CHAPTER IV.

AFTER leaving the French man-of-war, the submarine travelled for some hours at a depth of about thirty feet, and when she again rose to the surface it was early morning.

Some way ahead of them lay Plymouth, and this they passed at full speed on the surface of the water.

A liner from the Cape, with a number of invalided and time-expired soldiers, passed, the peculiar form of the "Nautilus" exciting much attention.

Bob tied a long bamboo along one of the deck stanchions, and upon this he hoisted a Union Jack, on seeing which the Tommies gave three hearty cheers, and Bob responded to the utmost of his powers.

At Plymouth they came across a fleet of fishing-smacks engaged in their craft.

One of these boats, with its brown sail glowing warm in the rays of the morning sun, was drifting two miles and more away from its companions, and, as the "Nautilus" approached, her crew could hear shouts and screaming.

At Bob's request, backed by Sir Peter's orders, Captain Deane sent his vessel after the smack.

As they approached, the screams and cries became louder.

A boy was shouting for mercy, while one of the fishermen was lashing him heavily, so that the sound of the blows could be plainly heard.

Stripped to the waist, and tied by his wrists to the rigging, was a thin, starved-looking lad, while a fierce-looking man thrashed him.

The four others on board the smack were standing aloof, with sullen faces, as though they would have helped the boy, had they dared to do so.

The bully looked up as the "Nautilus" came quietly alongside, and Captain Deane hailed:

"What is the matter there?"

"You mind your own business," replied the bully.

"What's the matter, youngster?" cried out Sir Peter to the lad.

The boy was gasping, and though he evidently made an effort to answer, only an inarticulate sound escaped his lips.

"I'll teach you to interfere with what do'ant consarn you," shouted the fisherman. "This here's a mutineer, and I'm giving him discipline," and, raising the knotted rope, he brought it down with terrific force across the bruised shoulders of the unfortunate lad.

This time no cry escaped from the pale lips; the boy had fainted.

"Uncle, Gil, I cannot stand that," cried Bob, furiously. "I am going for that brute! Captain Deane, please put the ship closer alongside."

Bob was evidently not the only one who thought of stopping the brute's tyranny, for Captain Deane ran the "Nautilus" close to the smack, and Bob, Gilbert, and two men jumped on board.

The tyrant aimed a blow at them, but, almost before it could take effect, he was thrown struggling to the ground, calling in vain to his men to help him.

His assailants quickly bound his hands and feet together, and then, cutting the unfortunate boy clear of the rigging, they carried him, still fainting, on board, where the steward attended to him.

"We ought to give this blackguard a hundred lashes!" cried Bob, indignantly.

"Leave me to deal with him when we reach England again," cried Sir Peter. "A man like this has no right to command others; and though money is often wrongly used in this respect, this time it shall be used well in bringing him to justice."

"Now, lads," he said, addressing the crew of the smack, "take your vessel straight back to harbour, and report the facts of the case; and speak without fear or favour, for if, when I return, I find that any of you have been making a false statement, I will serve you the same as I shall serve this bully, and he shall shiver in the streets yet, and know what it is to want."

Once again on board the "Nautilus," Bob and his friends found that the lad had recovered from his faint sufficiently to thank them all for what they had done for him.

"Put me on shore anywhere, gentlemen," he cried. "If I cannot get work I must starve, but I don't mean to go back to that wretch. He has killed one apprentice already, and he would have killed me before another month was out."

It really seemed true, for the lad not only was knocked about, but he was starved to emaciation.

"Would you like to go with us?" asked Sir Peter. "Boy's wages and kind treatment?"

"If you please, sir," answered the lad, "I would come for no wages at all if I could be treated kindly, and I'm sure I would do anything for you gents."

"I warn you, my lad, that we are going on a very dangerous voyage. Every man on board this ship is aware that he may never come back. This is a submarine vessel, and goes under the sea."

The boy's eyes opened wide.

"That's my luck turned sir," he cried, gleefully. "It is the very thing that I have wanted to ship in. I do want to see where them mermaids live."

"What's your name?" asked Gilbert.

"Bill Yeo, sir, at your service," said the boy.

And so Bill was shipped, and in a little time he began to look the smart young sailor that he was.

Through the chops of the Channel, and bearing west-sou'-west, the "Nautilus" sped, sometimes above water, and sometimes below, until land was no longer in sight, and only a vast expanse of blue water was to be seen, moving in heavy rollers like tumbling mountains.

The following morning was passed at gun and rifle practice, and Bob was delighted to find how well he could aim with the little Mauser.

The second night after leaving land, Bob, Gilbert, and Sir Peter were on deck; the two elders were smoking, whilst the youngster, awed into silence by the darkness, sat listening to the washing of the waves as they smote the sides of the swiftly moving "Nautilus." There was no moon, but the stars seemed nearer than Bob had ever noticed them before.

Members of the crew who were off duty were sitting or lolling about, and were talking softly among themselves.

In the far distance could be seen a light, which approached them nearer every minute, until from a glimmering star it was seen to be a headlight of some large vessel.

Then, as she came nearer, she seemed on fire, as the lights streamed through her every port.

"A large liner, that, sir, making for England," said Captain Deane. "Would you like me to speak her, Sir Peter?"

"I should. I have a letter, and should like to send it home," was the reply.

The "Nautilus" sped quietly towards the leviathan, showing a riding light such as is carried by a fishing vessel when at anchor.

As she approached, Captain Deane hailed.

"What steamer is that?" he shouted.

They were near enough to hear cries of alarm on board, and hurried conversations.

"The 'Kaiser,'" was the reply. "You have already given us your word that you would not molest us again," called out someone from the bridge of the big vessel.

"What does he mean?" asked Sir Peter. "Hail him again. Tell him we want him to take a letter."

The "Nautilus" drew alongside the steamer, and kept pace with her until an officer came to the side and looked over at them.

"We had your word that you would not molest us again," the man shouted.

"What do you mean? We have not spoken you before," called back Captain Deane.

"Oh, yes, you have, and we paid you," cried the man.

"Uncle," cried Bob, "he means the other submarine. Try him!"

"Have you seen a submarine like ours lately?" called out Gilbert Romer.

"We saw you, and it's no use your trying your tricks on with us. We have given you all the specie we have on board, and we have no more."

"We have only just left England," cried Sir Peter. "We are after the submarine that you saw the other day. Please tell us when and where you saw her, and all particulars. Has she been committing piracy on you?"

"What nation are you?" shouted another officer, coming up, who proved to be the captain of the liner.

"British," shouted Bob, before the others could answer; "all of us Britishers to the backbone."

There was another hurried talk among those on board the "Kaiser," and then the great steamer slowed down, while the captain leaned over the bridge to speak to them, turning on the searchlight in order to get a better look at them.

"Yes, you are certainly not the monsters we met the other day. They called their craft the 'Boer Privateer,' but they are nothing but pirates. We had to pay them nearly six thousand pounds in cash, and they threatened that if we reported this when we got back that they would sink us next voyage, and every vessel in our line. We thought it was them again."

"When did you see them last?" asked Sir Peter.

"Two days ago," and the captain gave them the latitude and the longitude.

"Will you be good enough to say nothing of having seen us, and be kind enough to take this letter and post it when you reach Southamp-

ton?" and Sir Peter threw the note on board.

"If we can find that privateer, you and your line will be able to sail in peace in future. Good-night, captain."

"There," said Bob, turning to his companions, "was I not right through all, and didn't I tell you that the Boers had a submarine? I said that it was that which sunk the 'Aurora,' and I believe that 'Beth and Marjory are prisoners with these Boer privateers."

"Let's hope that is the worst," said Gilbert.

CHAPTER V.

It was early morning, and the weather cold, and the sea misty grey, when Bob came up from below, the "Nautilus" being now working at her usual half-speed on the surface.

Some hours had passed since they had spoken the German steamer, and how far in front of them was the Boer submarine they had yet no idea.

That she existed, and was committing piracy on the high seas, they had now no doubt; that she had already done great damage they were sure.

Probably every day would cost Britain tens of thousands of pounds, as she sunk the best of her vessels.

It was chilly on deck, the grey mist wetting like a soft rain, and Bob had to walk sharply up and down to keep himself warm.

Presently he was joined by his uncle, and then by Captain Deane, and lastly Sir Peter made his appearance and asked when breakfast would be ready.

"This seafaring life gives me a fine appetite," he said. "I feel that I could eat a shark steak now, I am so hungry."

"I think I could eat the whole shark,' said Bob, laughing, and Captain Deane said solemnly:

"If I had known Bob beforehand, I'd have victualled for another six men," at which all laughed.

"I can smell bacon," said Bob as

he leaned over the hatchway, and down below the cook, on his patent electric stove, was frying the bacon for the meal.

"What did we come up for?" asked Bob. "It is much more interesting under the sea. When the light shines from our porthole windows all sorts of fish come and run their noses against us."

"We came up," said Captain Deane, "firstly in order to recharge our stores of oxygen, and we kept above water in order to economise our petrol. You see, Bob, we can go almost as fast again on the surface with only half the consumption."

"I shall be glad when we can put on our diving suits," said Bob, "and go for a walk at the bottom."

"That we can only do, my boy," said Sir Peter, "when the bottom is not far down from the surface. However, you shall have an opportunity soon."

"And breakfast is ready," said Captain Deane, as the electric gong rang, and Bob, forgetting all about diving-suits, hurried below.

Towards the afternoon some experiments in diving and steering under water were conducted, the lantern pictures showing what few surrounding objects there were.

It was while looking intently at the screen on which these pictures were shown that a formless mass, like a huge blot, was thrown dully on the sheet.

"That looks like rocks ahead," said Captain Deane, who was watching intently, and steering from a little apparatus like the keyboard of a piano.

"It isn't a whale, is it?" asked Bob.

"It is too far off us to see clearly what it may be," answered the skipper. "We shall know in a minute."

Then, as the "Nautilus" drew nearer, the object took shape.

First, in blurred outline, could be seen what was undoubtedly the hull of a vessel, and then three stumps of broken masts.

They neared her slowly, until the lights from the ports showed her plainly at only a few yards' distance.

"There, look at that—that hole in her,' said Bob, excitedly; and surely in her side was a great rent through which the water streamed.

She was a barque of some 3000 tons register, sunken 300 feet below the surface, lying on her side as she had fallen over when the rush of waters had entered her.

She was still slowly sinking, and would continue to do so until the density of the water increased so that it destroyed her.

Sir Peter looked inquiringly at Captain Deane.

"Yes, Sir Peter, that is the work of a ram. I should say that the privateer has done this thing," said the skipper.

"Can we board her and see what there is?" asked Bob.

"It's too risky," answered the captain. "I should say that the vessel has been boarded and pillaged first, and sunk afterwards when the crew had either been taken away or got rid of."

"How terrible!" said Gilbert; "and it may be that there are fifty British vessels like this one destroyed by the enemy."

"They have no chance," put in Sir Peter. "It is not war, it is simply massacre. But we shall find the destroyer yet."

"And then my Mauser shall speak," said Bob.

The "Nautilus" was now turned from the sad spectacle and headed almost south, and in order to hasten her she was brought to the surface again.

The sinking sun was just quivering on the verge of the horizon, where it hung for some moments as it departed.

No twilight followed, but in a few moments the stars came out, and the night was upon them.

Presently the moon rose, and threw a silver lane along the waters, on either side of which was a wall of darkness.

It was from out this darkness into the silver stream that a small, dark object was seen.

Bob, always on the look-out, saw it first with his keen eyes, and pointed it out to Captain Deane, who steered the submarine directly towards it.

"It seems to me to be a ship's boat," he said. "Whether or not there is anyone in her we cannot see yet."

"Perhaps it is someone escaped from the ship we saw down below," suggested Bob.

"Perhaps so, my lad. There is many a boat sets sail on these broad seas that is never heard of again."

The "Nautilus" drew nearer, and her crew saw an idle sail flapping against the mast.

There was no one at the tiller, and the boat yawed in unsteady fashion as they crept alongside.

Some dark forms were at the bottom of the craft, which was awash, huddled beneath coats, and there was no reply to Captain Deane's rousing hail.

"Jump in, Robson," he said to a herculean engineer, who was watching with them, and the man quickly entered, the boat swaying as he touched it.

He stepped down, and lifted the coats, and then called out:

"There are three of them here, captain. Two are alive, but I don't know about the other."

"Pass them on board, Robson—gently, now—and we will have them attended to."

And almost immediately three lifeless forms were carried on board the "Nautilus," and taken below to be wrapped in hot blankets, and to receive the attention of the steward and Gilbert, who knew something about restoratives.

The boat was allowed to drift away after she had been cleared.

Then, later, it was discovered that one of the rescued sailors was out of his mind, and was shouting incoherently; another was shivering with an ague, until his berth shook with him; but the other was white and silent: the rescue had come too late for him.

It was twenty-four hours before the two men recovered at all, and then from one of them they learnt that he was lately captain of the trading steamer the "Thomas and Mary," that owing to yellow fever he had lost some of the crew, and others had deserted him, and that at San Francisco he had been obliged to ship a mixed crew of Lascars, Portuguese, and riff-raff. These had shown signs of mutiny when they were only three days out, but he had unwisely disregarded the signs, and one night they rose, killed the first and second mates and the carpenter, and he and the boatswain and a passenger—the one who was now lying dead—had made their escape in the little boat which they had just left.

They had only a couple of biscuits and no water, and they thought that the end had come, for they were too far gone to know of their rescue when it was made.

"Would it not be a good thing to sink the blackguards who have got the steamer?" said Bob.

"We have other work to do, Bob," said Gilbert Romer. "Do not forget that those we love are waiting and hoping through the long days of darkness to see us again."

"Still, if we happened to run across the mutineers," persisted the lad, "we might fight them and get the ship back for the captain."

"You will have plenty of fighting before we have finished this voyage, I expect," Sir Peter's deep voice said. "Still, if we should happen on the 'Thomas and Mary' we will do our best to retake her."

Bob said nothing more on the subject to Sir Peter, but spoke to Captain Deane, with the result that very soon the "Nautilus" shifted her course two points south, and again two points south, and a few hours later still again two points, making the segment of a circle.

Captain Deane was looking out for the "Thomas and Mary," for he had a very kind fellow-feeling for a brother skipper nearly murdered by his men.

It was some two hours after midnight, and Bob was in his berth dreaming of shooting Boers with his Mauser and slaying thousands of foes, when he was aroused by a hand placed on his shoulder.

"We have found the steamer that our friend on-board commanded," said Captain Deane's voice. "I am going to run alongside and try and capture her before she knows of our presence. It strikes me that there is a bad watch kept."

Bob dressed, and came on deck; and, as they drew nearer, those on board the "Nautilus" could hear shouts and singing.

It was evident that the mutineers were making merry.

Probably they had got at the spirits, which Captain Viney, their late master, stated were in the main hold.

Sir Peter and Gilbert were now awakened, and they agreed to endeavour to rush the mutineers as quickly as possible; and to this end they armed themselves and about a dozen of the most stalwart of the crew.

Captain Viney, despite his great weakness, insisted upon going with them, having borrowed a revolver, and very soon the "Nautilus" glided closer alongside the black hull of the steamer.

The sound as iron grated upon iron caused the mutineers to cease their merriment, and two or three looked over the side and instantly gave the alarm.

At the same time, Bob, Gilbert, and half-a-dozen of their fellows had climbed over the side, and were firing on the advancing crowd, who came rushing from below and from aft.

Evidently the mob of ruffians were prepared for an attack, for they carried firearms and other weapons with them, and a regular fusilade, for-

"CAPTAIN BALLANCE FELLED THE BOER, AND OBTAINED POSSESSION OF HIS RIFLE."

tunately ill-directed, met the gallant little band that faced them.

Gilbert had his yachting-cap shot from his head, while another bullet passed through his jacket without hurting him.

On the other side, several of the mutineers were seen to fall; but, mad drunk as most of them were, this did not deter them.

One wild-looking fellow with a marlinspike sprang forward, and was about to strike Gilbert down, when a shot from the bulwarks, on which Captain Viney had climbed, sent him staggering back.

Then an iron bar hurled at them struck Bob on the chest, and he fell against the coamings of the main hatch, where he lay, with all the breath knocked out of him.

There was hand-to-hand fighting now, and the mutineers were getting the best of it, although the men of the " Nautilus " only gave way inch by inch.

One of them was seized by three or four Lascars and hurled overboard, and it was going ill with the little band, when there came a ringing hurrah from the stern of the steamer, as Sir Peter, Captain Deane, and another party of men came hurrying to the assistance of their comrades.

They feared to fire, lest their bullets should harm friend as well as foe, and for some moments there was a terrible *mêlée*, in which Sir Peter, throwing away the cutlass he had been carrying, knocked down a couple of men with his fists.

Gilbert was facing a huge fellow, whom it afterwards turned out was the leader of the mutineers, and who was armed with a great bar of iron. from which Gilbert had already had several narrow escapes as the man swung it fiercely at his foe.

They were nearly at the forecastle now, and Gilbert stooped swiftly as a blow was aimed at his head.

The bar, missing him, struck the iron bulwark of the fo'castle and rebounded.

Then was Gilbert's chance.

He sprang forward, and, with the muzzle of his revolver, thrust the fellow a heavy blow in the face.

A Lascar came to the man's rescue, but a shot laid him low, and then came the giant mutineer's turn.

Running from his victorious enemy, half-stunned, he tumbled against a man almost as big as himself—Robson, the big engineer—who, promptly seizing him in his arms, threw him with violence on to the iron deck, where he was easily secured.

After the fall of their leader the mutineers lost heart.

Some of them were chased below; others tried to escape aloft, and these were shot; but in ten minutes all who remained alive were in irons, save five who were severely wounded, and who were placed in their bunks to be attended to.

Bob, who had recovered his breath, was in at the last struggle, and to such good purpose. that when all had assembled on deck Sir Peter took from his fob pocket his gold repeater and handed it to the boy, saying :

" This is for a lad who will *not* be beaten."

The " Nautilus " had lost one man killed, one dangerously wounded, who afterwards recovered, and several others more or less severely injured.

The man who had been thrown overboard had swum to the " Nautilus," but the victory had been hardly won.

Captain Viney was installed on board his own vessel, with a few of the " Nautilus's " crew to help him, and with instructions to follow the submarine as she again headed for the south-west.

Next day they met a steamer, the captain of which gladly lent a few men, so that the " Nautilus's " men could return to their own ship.

Captain Viney took a grateful farewell of his friends, and in due time reached port, where some of the mutineers were hanged and the others imprisoned.

CHAPTER VI.

BILL YEO, who had now recovered much of his health and strength, attached himself to Bob.

He was Bob's most obedient army, and Bob, a strict, though kind, captain, ordered him about in correct military style.

The two boys were always together, generally in mischief, Captain Deane said, although in their mischief there was no great harm.

They were both alike in their desire for knowledge, and their greatest anxiety was to put on the diving-suits and to explore the bed of the ocean, Bill having a firm belief that pearls grew down there like the currants on the bushes in his mother's garden in Cornwall.

Sometimes the boys would amuse themselves by the hour together firing at a target that they had rigged aft, with Bob's Mauser, or with a revolver, so that both became quite good shots, and Bob. with great pride, showed a piece of cardboard as big as his hand with the figure "4" perforated in shot-holes.

Gilbert Romer, with Sir Peter's permission, instituted a series of shooting prizes, in which all competed, and Bob was delighted when he obtained second prize with a score of 100 out of 105 points, while to his inextinguishable joy Bill Yeo came in seventh with a score of eighty-four.

It was in the chilly first grey streaks of early dawn that the lookout gave the warning cry, "Sail ho!"

Bob, who was up early, was soon eagerly on the look-out, with Bill beside him.

A vessel, black and scarred, was lying some two miles away on the port bow, and the "Nautilus" was heading toward her.

As she approached, they saw no signs of life on board the derelict; the rigging was burnt away; a few pieces of charred sail clung to the masts; the paint upon her sides rose in great blisters where it had not already fallen.

There had been a fire at sea, one of the most terrible of all disasters that can overtake a vessel far from land.

Captain Deane had decided to pass on, when Bob entreated him to run alongside so that he and Bill could go on board and see if there was anything worth taking away; and the good-natured captain had the "Nautilus" run close enough to enable the youngsters to board the derelict.

"What's that?" said Bob, suddenly. "It sounds like a dog."

Bill threw himself down on the charred deck, placing his ear to the floor.

"It is a dog down below," he cried. "Perhaps there are people there, too."

The sound came from aft, but all the hatches were off, as though the ship had been pillaged and her cargo thrown overboard.

Following the sound, they went down the cabin stairs and into the cabin.

This, too, was in confusion; papers were strewn about the floor, a broken desk lay upon the ground, some empty wine bottles were overturned upon the table.

The two lads looked into the berths; these were all empty, but all bore the same signs of pillage and destruction.

The barking sounded louder as Bob called out:

"Good dog, good boy!"

"It is down the lazarette," said Bill; and, diving under the cabin table, he pulled aside the carpet and disclosed a small trap-door.

The dog whined painfully, and Bob, striking a light, called out:

"It is a great Newfoundland, and he is so weak he can hardly stand."

Bill cut a rope and passed it round the poor animal, and they hauled it up; it wagged its bushy tail, and vainly tried to stand, and greedily lapped up some water that Bill fetched for it.

"I wonder how he got down there," said Bob. "You are sure there is no one else below?"

"Certain, sure!" said Bill. "I rather fancy that somebody hit him on the head and threw him down there. Poor brute! and ain't 'e 'ungry!" and Bill threw the dog a ship's biscuit.

The boys carried him on board the "Nautilus," and christened him on the spot "Waif," and "Waif" was at once installed a member of the ship's company.

Bill picked up a few odds and ends from the burnt vessel, and then it was abandoned, to be sunk by the first merciless storm it might encounter.

"It is probable that it has been set on fire," said Captain Deane, "and a heavy rainstorm has prevented more than the damage we have seen. What the reason was, we cannot tell. It is possible that it is a case which may interest the insurance companies not a little," and he entered in his log particulars of the ship's name, number, and so on, as sailors are bound to report, and once more the "Nautilus" proceeded on her voyage.

During the next two days nothing unusual occurred, excepting that they witnessed at sea a fight between two huge bull whales.

The great creatures lashed the sea in their fury, and rushed at each other with open mouths, each endeavouring to fasten on to his enemy's open jaw.

Sometimes they disappeared from sight, as they carried the fight to the lowest depths; sometimes they would spring to the surface so quickly that half of their huge bodies leaped above the water, and fell back with a splash that could be heard far away.

Bob wanted to have a shot at them with his Mauser, but Captain Deane explained to him that his bullets would not be felt by them more than he himself would feel a pin-prick, for, encased as they were in a covering of blubber, they were almost impervious to the bullets of the military rifles, and so, reluctantly, Bob gave over his idea of whaling.

One day they passed through a swarm of squid, some of these large enough to have pulled a man under.

Great hideous creatures they were, with their arms that tried to cling to the glass portholes, and at night, when the light shone through the ports, they came alongside in thousands, so that Bill acknowledged feeling quite relieved when they were no longer in sight.

Next day they passed some wreckage, a hen coop, a spare yard, a few planks, and then a couple of hatches belonging to some vessel.

Captain Deane cruised round, but there were no signs of a wreck, but then more wreckage floated along, including a boat, keel upwards.

They brought it alongside, and Bob was the first to see upon it the name s.s. "Aurora."

"Uncle! Uncle!" he cried. "See here. This is a boat belonging to the 'Aurora.' She must have been sunk here."

"I do not think so," said Captain Deane, thoughtfully, as Gilbert rushed up, almost breathless with excitement. "This wreckage has been travelling with the Gulf Stream. The 'Aurora' must have been sunk a long way from here. Still, we are evidently on the track, and we may find more wreckage from time to time to guide us if we keep a sharp look-out."

There were plenty eager for this work, for all knew the tale of the sunken "Aurora," and Gilbert himself was never weary.

For two days they followed the same course, now and again meeting evidence of the wreck—now a chest, sometimes an oar, sometimes merely planks, which might indeed have belonged to any craft.

Then it was that Captain Deane sought Sir Peter and Gilbert.

"I have a theory, gentlemen," he said. "Most of the wreckage would float at the rate of a mile an hour, twenty-four miles a day. Judging as nearly as we can the time when the 'Aurora' disappeared, we should now be near the spot where she sunk. I now propose to search under the sea, and to keep our X-ray apparatus in constant use. I propose to work in four-mile circles."

This was agreed to, and now the "Nautilus" began her submarine voyage in earnest, passing nearly the whole of the twenty-four hours below the surface.

For five days no signs of the wreck were seen, and anxious hearts were beginning to lose hope of ever finding those they sought, when one afternoon, shortly after sunset, the screen of the magic lantern showed a dim mass.

They hurried forward to this, and found the water shoaling up to it.

A huge mountain, projecting from the bed of the ocean to within fifty feet of the surface, cragged and rocky, stood before them, with chasms here and there that yawned blackly as the "Nautilus" passed them by.

Beyond the mountain lay a deep valley, and then another huge pile of rocks reared itself higher than the Himalayas.

This was evidently part of a chain of submarine mountains that would have dwarfed any mountains known on land.

Still skirting the rocks, with the X-rays disclosing picture after picture of rugged scenery, where seaweeds and anemones took the place of Alpine flowers and plants, the "Nautilus" sped on, until Gilbert, with an exclamation, drew attention to a shadowy picture now to be seen.

"Only rocks, Mr. Romer," said Captain Deane. "They take queer shapes sometimes."

"I do not think so," said Gilbert, anxiously. "I could swear that that was the funnel of a steamer."

"We will go back and search," said the skipper, good-naturedly; "but you will find you are mistaken."

The "Nautilus" cautiously swung round, and approached nearer to the side of the mountain, the picture on the screen becoming larger and clearer.

"It is—it is a funnel!" cried Bob; "whether it is the 'Aurora' or not, there is a steamer sunk on that mountain."

"I believe you are right, my lad," said Captain Deane. "I am sure you are," he added, a moment later, and there, on an edge, with her back broken, lay a great steamer, her funnel still upright.

No word was spoken among the little group as Captain Deane cautiously steered past the bows of the sunken vessel, so that the searchlight fell full upon her.

Yes! there was the name, with the paint still white and clear, "Aurora."

They had found her at last!

CHAPTER VII.

Long and silently Gilbert Romer gazed on the forsaken steamer that had so lately been the home of her whom he loved best in all the world.

Bob, not as usual merry and talkative, stood by his side, another silent watcher of the great mystery that they were trying to fathom.

Captain Deane first broke the silence.

"We have been very fortunate in happening upon the very spot where the steamer lies. I think now will be the time to use our diving-suits, and to make what search we can on board that vessel. There is some danger in going over a sunken ship, and I think that if two risk their lives it will be quite sufficient. I intend to be one of the two."

"And I, the other, please, captain," said Gilbert Romer eagerly.

"Yes," said Sir Peter, "I think that is your privilege; but I think that I must put my veto on Captain Deane's going. He is our guide, and I do not think we ought to allow him to take any risk."

"Let me go instead," pleaded Bob. "I am strong and active, and I will keep close to Uncle Gil the whole time."

Captain Deane vainly urged that he could not allow anyone to march into danger unless he were beside him, but the gallant old skipper was out-voted, and in the end it was agreed that Bob and his uncle should make the adventure.

The diving suits were brought out,

and both were encased in them, their heads in great helmets with goggle eyes, and boots with leaden soles, weighing pounds, holding down their feet.

The air reservoirs were carried in several small chambers hung around the waist, so that in case of accident to one another was available, the suits being self-contained, and independent of the usual pump.

The 'Nautilus" was so arranged that those in the conning-tower could be shut off from the rest of the vessel, and so Gilbert and his nephew stood therein and waited while the platform below them was bolted and screwed.

Then, at a given signal, they unfastened the screws of the hatch above the conning-tower, and allowed the water to rush in.

Bob could feel the chill of it creeping up him, and there was buzzing in his ears as the air came rushing too quickly into the helmet.

However, this he soon found ways to remedy; and seeing his uncle move up the ladder, he climbed after him, surprised and pleased that his heavily-weighted boots no longer held him to the floor as they had done before the water was round him.

The "Nautilus" was run against the bows of the "Aurora," so that it was easy to climb down a rope ladder and board the sunken ship.

"Oh! uncle, supposing we find them on board!" said Bob, suddenly, fear-struck as he thought of the awful possibility, and forgetting for the moment that his voice could not be heard by anyone but himself.

Gilbert was making straight for the cabins aft, and to gain these a chasm of about ten feet, caused by the breaking of the vessel, had to be crossed, and here again the rope ladder had to be brought into use.

At length the after part of the ship was reached, and Bob followed his uncle down the cabin stairs which had been trod by the loved ones so many, many times.

His heart beat at such a rate that he could hardly breathe.

The electric submarine lamps which they carried were now switched on, for they were beyond the lights of the "Nautilus."

They looked round them in fear of a gruesome discovery, into every nook and corner, into the berths, and under them.

The cabins were empty, and scuttling across the floor were a number of crabs, and both searchers felt the relief so great, that simultaneously they faced each other and shook hands.

The in-coming rush of waters had forced open doors and portholes, and lifted the deck above so that the trunks of clothes, empty boxes, and other things floated in and out, and one of the tin trunks Bob recognised as belonging to 'Beth.

In addition to these there were quantities of miscellaneous cargo, which had drifted out of the hold, bales and cases, and odd iron utensils, that had escaped from their packing.

Carefully they looked around for papers, but the sea had evidently reduced these to a pulp long ago.

A chart-case with two charts in floated against the ceiling, but nothing that would throw any light on the mystery could be found, and slowly they retraced their steps, and once more regained their own vessel.

The hatch of the conning-tower was screwed on again, and when this was done the water in it was pumped out, and then the floor opened, and they were among their friends once more.

"Have you found anything?" was the anxious inquiry as soon as their helmets had been taken off.

"There are no human remains on board," was the answer; and Sir Peter exclaimed, "Thank God for that! Then there's a good chance of their having escaped, so that they may some day be restored to their friends."

"Thanks to you," said Gilbert; "for whether we find them or not, I shall never forget what you have done for them, and for us."

The "Nautilus" soon after rose to the surface of the water, and sped on towards Monte Video, which she reached four days later, anchoring just outside the harbour.

Captain Deane, accompanied by

Sir Peter and Gilbert, went ashore to call at the office of the British Consul, Mr. Pritchard, to whom they told the tale of their quest.

"If you are right," exclaimed Mr. Pritchard, "your theory will account for a matter that has been troubling us for some days. As you have been at sea lately, you will probably not have heard that two of our gunboats, H.M.S. 'Seagull' and H.M.S. 'Teuton,' have not been heard of, and are supposed to have foundered. His Majesty's cruiser 'St. George,' which you passed just now, is to leave to-night in search of the missing men-of-war. Possibly this Boer pirate is accountable for their disappearance."

"I expect that is so," said Sir Peter, gravely, " and, however smart the gunboat, she would have no chance whatever against such an unseen foe as the submarine."

"I am expecting Captain Ballance, of the 'St. George,' here every minute. Perhaps you would like to have a chat with him," suggested Mr. Pritchard, and at that minute the clerk announced the arrival of the gallant officer.

Mr. Pritchard introduced Sir Peter and his friends, and in a few words explained their mission and his own views of the disappearance of the gunboats.

"If such a vessel as the Boer privateer exists," said Captain Ballance, "it is quite possible that it has done the damage; but I can hardly believe that such a craft could leave Europe without the fact being known to the Admiralty."

Sir Peter then told him their adventure with the German liner.

"It certainly looks as if the Boers have such a craft afloat," said Captain Ballance; "and if that is the case, I shall have to keep a sharp look-out."

"I am afraid," said Gilbert, "that the sharpest look-out will not find the submarine, and if she once sights you, you are helpless."

"We must do our duty, sir," answered Captain Ballance firmly. "We can but do our best; but I think it will be my proper course to communicate with the Admiralty and state confidentially your story. I suppose you have no objection?"

"None at all," said Sir Peter; "but already Mr. Romer has told the Admiralty that he had reason to believe that the Boers have a submarine afloat, and the Admiralty people would not listen to him."

"You made a mistake, Mr. Romer," said Captain Ballance. "Instead of going to the Admiralty, you should have gone to Lord Charles Beresford. The people you saw were civilians, whose only knowledge of ships comes from an occasional investigation of an illustrated paper. Unfortunately, they are the men in power, and, like most Government officials, their great idea is to save themselves trouble. There is no doubt that we have a difficult task in front of us; still, the British Navy has never yet failed its country, and it will not be the fault of my ship's company if we do not succeed in destroying or capturing the enemy."

"I have a proposal to make to you, Captain Ballance," said Sir Peter. "That is, that we accompany you, if you will consider us as an unofficial tender to your vessel."

"Unofficially I accept your offer, Sir Peter," answered Captain Ballance. "Officially, of course, I cannot recognise an armed vessel that does not belong to any navy; but I can see that if we are to meet this destroyer on equal terms it will only be with the aid of such a vessel as your own."

That same evening the "St. George" proceeded to sea with the "Nautilus" in her wake, amid the wonderment of the crowd which had gathered to see the departure of the vessels.

CHAPTER VIII.

THE "St. George" was a fairly modern cruiser, steaming nineteen knots at full speed, and fourteen knots with half consumption of coal, and at this pace the "Nautilus" could pass her at any time, so long as she kept on the surface.

Under the water the resistance was too great to make fast headway, and so the rails were rigged on deck, and the submarine, for three days, remained above water.

The great Atlantic rollers sometimes towered above her and threatened to crash upon her deck, but buoyant as a cork, she rose on their huge swell, and sunk again into the next deep valley of tossing ocean, unscathed.

Bob and Bill Yeo were playing on the deck with the dog Waif, which had by now quite recovered its strength; they were teaching it to vault over a stick they held between them, and Waif entirely entered into the fun, barking furiously.

But the deck of the "Nautilus" was rounded, and, wet as it was, it was not easy to run about on.

For those who staidly marched about, as Sir Peter Patterson and Captain Deane were doing, it was safe enough, but when the two lads began chasing the dog, danger was not far ahead.

It was Bob who slipped first and slid over the side in a moment.

Bill Yeo immediately threw himself down and tried to reach his young master, and as he did so an in-coming wave caught him and swept him overboard.

The poor dog whined as he saw them carried astern, and a moment afterwards it had sprung after them.

Bob could swim a little, and after the first sudden shock he threw out his arms and legs, and managed to keep his head above water with a little exertion.

Bill, however, like many another boy who goes to sea, could hardly swim a stroke, and he was struggling frantically as the green water splashed into his open mouth.

"Help!" he cried in strangled tones, as he and Bob rose almost side by side on the crest of a great wave.

"Don't kick so," roared Bob. "Throw your arms and legs out and you will float."

But Bill, in his fright, instead of obeying these instructions, clutched hold of one of Bob's arms, and clung to it madly.

"Leave go, or we shall both be drowned!" spluttered Bob, and then, as another huge billow drew near, the two boys sunk beneath it.

A moment after they came up, Bill by now more than half unconscious, still, however, clinging to Bob; and the latter was beginning to lose hope of being rescued when a short, sharp bark just ahead told him that Waif had not forsaken them.

"Good dog!" he shouted, and then under the two boys went again.

Bob fought desperately to get to the surface.

This time Bill's weight seemed to drag him down—down—down!

He was bursting for want of air, and fighting desperately to clear himself from his encumbrance, when he felt himself lifted up above the water.

Waif was there, and had him firmly by the shoulder, and then, for a few minutes, the three remained together, while another wave kept them up.

Before this a boat had been lowered from the "St. George" and was making towards them, for the crew had seen the accident, and now the stalwart bluejackets were pulling hard to reach them, while the "Nautilus," which had no boat of her own, had turned, and was hurrying forward.

It was touch and go with Bill Yeo when the sailors pulled the unconscious boy on board, for both Bob and the dog were well-nigh spent; but some hot tea and blankets soon brought the youngsters round, and Bill was thoroughly ashamed of himself when he learned how nearly he had caused the death of his loved young master.

"I did not know it, Master Bob," he said, gravely, "or I would have gone down first," and Bob, who could quite understand that the boy's action was involuntary, accepted his apology.

The vessels were now approaching the region where the submarine privateer had last been heard of, and orders were given to show no lights at night.

Even below, where lights were necessary, they were not lighted until the portholes had been carefully blocked so that not a gleam could be seen from outside.

It was even difficult for the " Nautilus " at times to keep near the other vessel, which was steaming on almost unseen; but, whereas some light showed from the funnel, which was just sufficient to guide the " Nautilus " when but a little distance away, the submarine showed no light at all, having no funnel.

It was a triumph of the new motor power over steam.

The Boer privateer must have sighted the " St. George " without her having seen them, for she carried no light by which the British man-o'-war could track her.

But for a piece of sheer good luck the " St. George " would have been sunk, as no doubt the two vessels she was searching for had been destroyed.

It was early morning, with dark, heavy clouds hiding the moon and stars.

The " Nautilus " was lying about 200 yards away from the " St. George," keeping a parallel course at her side, with this interval between them.

Bob, who insisted on taking his watch, was on deck with two of the men, when he thought he heard a slight disturbance in the sea as of water breaking on a rock or against the bow of a ship.

He looked intently into the darkness, and through the gloom there suddenly loomed a great shadow making straight towards them at a slight angle.

" That is the Boer privateer racing after the ' St. George.' "

Bob pointed her out to the second officer, who was in charge, and he at once edged nearer to the " St. George," so as to keep the " Nautilus " between the British man-o'-war and the privateer, while Bob ran down and roused up Captain Deane, Sir Peter, and his uncle.

The privateer was stealing closer and closer to the cruiser, the lookout of which seemed as yet to be unaware of the presence of the " Nautilus."

" Couldn't we sink her now? " whispered Bob, eagerly. " One shot or one torpedo would do it."

" And then how should we discover where the Boers have taken our friends? " asked his uncle, in a low tone.

" You are quite right, Mr. Romer," said Captain Deane. " Our business now is to frighten the Boer away and then follow her. I am going to disclose ourselves now."

The privateer was now not fifty yards away, still just a black blot on the water, but showing a white track behind her.

Suddenly the " Nautilus " threw a searchlight full upon her, and almost instantly she dived, probably thinking the light came from the cruiser.

Those on deck of the " Nautilus " hurried below, and in less than half a minute the hatch of the conning-tower was screwed down, and the vessel was hurriedly dipping under water to take up a position beneath the " St. George."

Her searchlight now illuminated the sea for 100 yards round, while the X-rays showed the Boer running parallel.

By this time the privateer must have been aware that a submarine accompanied the British man-o'-war.

" Ah! they have begun," said Captain Deane, suddenly pressing hard upon the keyboard by which he steered the " Nautilus," and on the lantern screen a small object could be seen leaving the privateer and approaching them.

The " Nautilus " immediately swerved and dived as a torpedo came swiftly towards them.

It missed by a few yards and was lost in the sea beyond.

Again the Boers tried to torpedo the " Nautilus," and again they missed.

And then Captain Deane, with a swift turn, got just in the rear of the enemy, the beak of the " Nautilus " being close to the screw of the privateer.

"You see," he said to Sir Peter, "her torpedo tubes are all forward. She cannot fire at us aft while we are under water, and here we will remain."

The capabilities of the two vessels were now severely tried.

Swiftly the privateer turned, but not so swiftly but that the "Nautilus" kept close behind her.

Then she dived, and still her opponent was close beside her.

She dived still deeper, but Captain Deane was frightened of no depths.

She tried her speed against the "Nautilus," but the latter was the swifter boat and would not be left behind.

To port and to starboard she dodged, but always with the same result, the beak of the "Nautilus" was still within a few feet of her screw, nor could she in any way lengthen the distance between them.

It was evident that the Boers were becoming alarmed.

It would have been easy for the "Nautilus" to have run into their screw and strip it of its blades, and so leave them helpless.

No doubt they wondered that she did not do so, for then their capture would have been certain; and probably because she did not harm them, but remained stolidly astern, the motive of those who pursued seemed more mysterious than ever.

"The 'St. George' should be safe now," said Bob, after some two hours of this manœuvre.

"She should be," said Captain Deane, "for we are heading due south, and she is going north-west. Our friends the Boers evidently cannot make us out."

"But they'd be sure to run away when they'd met their match," said Bob.

"Yes," replied the captain; "but remember, that a Boer is always cunning. We have not finished with them yet."

"No!" said Sir Peter; "but they have this advantage over us, that they can destroy us, but we may not, for our own sakes, destroy them."

CHAPTER IX.

ONLY when the privateer rose to the surface did the "Nautilus" take in her supply of fresh air.

The Boers were very quick at this work, and, being prepared for it, and choosing their own time, they had the British vessel at a disadvantage.

It was monotonous work, this continual chase under water, when only the vessel in front was to be seen.

Bob grew restless under the forced inaction, and longed for active strife.

For the whole of one day the Boers kept under at a depth of one hundred fathoms before rising.

When the "Nautilus" followed suit, and the hatch was lifted, Bob rushed impetuously on deck to get a mouthful of fresh air.

"We're ashore," he called out, and the others hurried after him, surprised by his words.

"We're afloat," said Captain Deane, as he looked round, "and a

long way from land. This is the Sargossa Sea."

Just ahead, almost covered with green weed, was the privateer, her crew busily employed in clearing it away.

All around for miles was a mass of seaweed, that certainly gave the sea the appearance of a green field, so thick it was.

The Boers were swarming on their vessel, working very hard, seeming to take no heed of the "Nautilus," save for a sentry, who, with rifle in hand, watched.

"You can run," shouted Bob to them, unable to repress himself.

"Yah! and we can shoot ven der time coomes," the sentry yelled back.

"Come, Bob, that won't do. You mustn't speak to them," said his uncle, sternly.

"Go below," Sir Peter ordered him angrily; and Bob, grinning, went into the cabin and took out his

Mauser, which he carefully loaded, after which he stationed himself inside the conning-tower, just out of sight.

"Vat you vant?" roared a huge Boer across the narrow space between the vessels.

"Are you prepared to ransom your captives?" asked Sir Peter.

"Have you any ladies among them, the Miss Grants?" called out Gilbert Romer.

A loud laugh answered this question, and one of the Boers translated the inquiries to those who spoke only Taal.

"We will pay you well," cried Sir Peter, persuasively.

"You bay us! Ve dake all ve vant. Ve dake all your dirty Englishers' money. Ve dake you all prisoners. You dirty Englishers shall be our slaves. Ve conquer you now," bellowed the big Boer, and, as he spoke, his comrades, excepting the sentry, climbed below like so many bears.

Then, with a derisive laugh, the big leader went below, too, and the sentry slowly followed him.

It was at this minute that Bob put his head above the hatch of the conning-tower.

He saw the sentry go below, and then noticed that his rifle did not disappear with him, but that the muzzle was pointed at the "Nautilus."

Hardly daring to breathe, he threw forward his little Mauser, aiming about six inches above the spot where the Boer's rifle lay on the edge of the privateer's hatchway.

Suddenly the head of the Boer slowly showed itself as he took aim at the group on board the "Nautilus," and at the same moment Bob pulled his trigger.

There was a double report, but the Boer's bullet went skyward, as its owner fell below, shot through the head.

There was a cry of surprise on board the "Nautilus," for those on deck were hardly prepared for such treachery, and Gilbert caught a glimpse of the ruffian's head just at the moment that Bob fired.

"I've hit him!" cried Bob, step-ping on to the deck, and loading as he did so.

"You've saved the life of one of us," said Sir Peter, calmly; "but you should obey orders, Bob, at all costs. A good soldier must do that."

Bob blushed—he had not yet got over that habit.

"I saw the beggar was going to fire," he said.

"You should not have been there to see. Go below, now," and Sir Peter turned away, while Bob, abashed, went into the cabin and began cleaning his Mauser.

He had expected praise instead of blame; he thought that he had done well, and that Sir Peter was ungrateful.

"Weren't you rather hard on him, Sir Peter?" Captain Deane said, when the lad had gone.

"Must teach a lad discipline. I had to learn, and in a rougher school than Bob is in now. But when he has learned the lesson, we'll make it up to him, eh, Deane? A little nest-egg of a thousand pounds won't hurt him, eh, Romer?"

"It's very good of you, Sir Peter," said Gilbert, who had been resenting silently what he thought was harsh treatment to his favourite nephew.

Now he understood the millionaire, and saw that he was right.

Obedience must be taught at all costs, for a lad who habitually disobeys will never learn to teach others to be obedient, and the battle of life is only won by obedience to higher orders.

In the hurry and bustle of the last few minutes no one had noticed the disappearance of the privateer.

She had sunk suddenly, and instant orders were given to clear the deck of the "Nautilus," which, in another moment, was sinking also.

But some of the weed had got round the propeller, so that it was difficult to move, and the searchlight did not show up the craft they were after.

The X-rays were at once turned on, and on the screen the blur of some large object was to be seen.

The "Nautilus" was turned towards it, but, as the propeller was clogged, only half of the usual speed could be maintained, and this was getting less.

The object soon proved to be merely a sunken hulk, water-soddened and naked, and no other picture was to be seen.

"This is serious," said Sir Peter. "If once the privateer gives us the slip, we may be a long time before finding her again."

"I ought to have kept a sharper look-out, Sir Peter," said Captain Deane. "I was to blame; but in the confusion——"

"We were all to blame, captain. But now, what are we to do?"

"Try a four-mile circle at limit depth," said the skipper; "but it's almost like looking for a needle in a bottle of hay."

"Another bit of Boer slimness," observed Sir Peter, bitterly: "and to think that I saw no ulterior motive when they tried that shot! I, at least, ought to have known that they counted on putting us in confusion and so escaping."

The "Nautilus" circled one way and then another, but no privateer was to be seen, and the disappointment was great.

Success had seemed so near, that it was very bitter to lose the chance at just the last moment.

"Let us try the surface for a moment," Sir Peter said, after nearly twelve hours of fruitless cruising.

"I am afraid we shall see nothing of her there, Sir Peter, but we'll make the experiment. She's slipped us, I fear," and Captain Deane, his fingers on the key-board, sent the bow of the great submarine vessel upward.

For a little while she rose slowly, the gauge showing the movement, then more slowly, and then she stopped.

"What's wrong?" asked Sir Peter, noticing the skipper's anxious face.

"Can't make out, Sir Peter, but we're not rising, and the screws are working."

He called through the tube for Mr. Buchan, the engineer, who promptly came.

"Anything gone wrong with your engines, Mr. Buchan?"

"No, sir; they are just fit for anything."

"Then what's holding us?" muttered the captain. "We'll try again," and now, obedient to his touch, the "Nautilus" sunk for a while.

"Now we'll see," he said, and sent her full speed upward.

The same result happened.

At first she rose quickly, then slowly, and then stopped.

"It's the weed," called out Bob, as he looked out at the nearest port-hole; and there, indeed, in dense masses, like the sudd of the Nile, lay the weed around them.

"We must rise somewhere else, that's all," said the captain, noticing the alarmed faces of those around him; and again he telegraphed the order for reversing the engines; but this time, in spite of repetition, the order was seemingly not carried out.

Buchan ran back to the engine-room, and returned again later with the news that the screws were fouled, and would not move.

The weed had thoroughly jammed them this time.

It was now a serious matter, for, unless they could get the "Nautilus" away from the weed, a certain and horrible death awaited them.

Captain Deane began to put on a diving-dress.

"I'll come with you, captain," said Bob, with his usual alertness.

"And I—and I," cried out the others.

"Too dangerous," said the skipper, abruptly. "This is my fault, and I'll take the risk."

"We are all concerned. I would rather risk my life than wait here," said Gilbert Romer.

"It's slippery work on the hull, and if one slips it's nearly a mile to the bottom, and no rising," said the captain.

"I'm like a monkey; I won't slip," said Bob, with a grin. "Besides, if there are enough of us, we can join hands, and the end one hold on to the stanchions which we can rig."

"Quite right, Bob. You're a smart boy," said Sir Peter, approvingly. "How many diving-suits have you, Deane?"

"Ten, sir, but only three at the most can leave the ship at one time."

"That'll do. We shall want all the ten. Buchan, send us five of your best men, and let's make a start."

Soon afterwards, Captain Deane, Buchan, and Bob were carefully climbing over the turtle-shaped back of the "Nautilus," fixing in the standards, with nearly a quarter of a mile of water pressing upon them, and three-quarters of a mile below them.

As Deane had said, one slip meant death, and death once came very near to the skipper, the slimy weed yielding to his foot, so that he slid downwards along the side.

But Buchan grabbed him in time, and, holding on to a stanchion which Bob was just fixing, he hauled him up.

It was an anxious moment, for the foot of the stanchion was not properly home, and if it gave way two lives, and not one, would be lost.

Bob clung to it, pushing it down with all his might, and it held, and then the two men shook hands.

It was so weird, this silence, under the circumstances, but that handshake meant much.

Presently three more divers appeared, and soon all ten were ready.

The stanchions were tested, and then, holding Buchan's hand with his left, and an axe in his right, the skipper began slowly to slip over the curve toward the stern. Others held Buchan's and each other's hands until a string of eight were attached to the iron stanchions which Bob and Sir Peter were holding down.

There was a jerk and a stiffening of the chain.

Deane had, as was feared, slipped again, but the human chain held, and he was pulled back and enabled to reach the screw.

Here the work was tedious, and two hours passed, every man getting stiff under the strain, yet each one knowing that if for one moment he relaxed his hold his comrades below him would probably be lost.

At last, as the air in the receivers became so foul that breathing was difficult, and men were panting, in some cases in agony, Captain Deane made an upward move.

Instantly the chain tightened again, it shortened by one man as the next nearest to the stanchions grasped it, then shortened again, until all stood together on the middle of the deck, and three entered the receiving chamber.

Willing hands below soon helped them out of their dresses, worn and white-faced men, two out of the three bleeding at the ears and nose.

Restoratives were administered to them, dazed and helpless as they were, and three more entered, and then last of all, Captain Deane, worthy leader of brave men.

Soon the engines were tried, the screws, after a little resistance, sped round, the "Nautilus" dived again, and then turned to leave the treacherous Sargossa Sea.

CHAPTER X.

A RUN of twelve hours, and then the skipper, still looking white and ill after his exertions, turned the bow of the submarine upwards once more.

This time there was no resistance, and a few minutes later all were breathing in the sweet air under the sky as they crowded upon the deck.

Around still lay the weed, but not in such dense masses.

The vessel was on the edge of the Sargossa, beyond which few vessels have penetrated, and fewer still returned to tell the tale.

There was no sign of the privateer.

She had vanished utterly, and there were despondent faces among those there.

Genial Bob was silent, and his uncle looked like a man from the grave.

Sir Peter whispered to Captain Deane.

"We found her once, and we shall find her again," said Sir Peter, breaking the silence at last.

Bob shook his head.

Gilbert made no movement, but sighed deeply.

"I think we had better make for Monte Video, and seek for news there," said Deane.

"Anything rather than give up the chase," replied Sir Peter; and so the head of the "Nautilus" was turned once more, and a few days later she anchored in the roads of La Plata.

Monte Video is 130 miles from Cape St. Mary, that forms the northern point of the entrance of the La Plata river, which, opposite the town, is some 30 miles wide.

The news the crew of the "Nautilus" learned was startling enough, and the vessels lying in the roadstead were full of it.

One of the boats of H.M.S. "St. George" had been picked up empty, together with other floating *débris*, which evidently told the tale that the splendid vessel had been lost at sea.

"That privateer meant to have her, and has done for her after all. Oh! how I would like to fight those Boers," cried Bob, his lethargy vanishing under the heat of his anger.

There was no doubt but that the "St. George" had gone down—there were no two opinions there; and the dread of the submarine was so great that some captains of the vessels anchored there could not persuade their crews to put to sea.

Captain Deane made notes of the position about where the floating *débris* had been found, and then hastily replenishing the ship's stores and water, the "Nautilus" started out to sea again within twenty-four hours after arrival.

"This must be about the place," he said, as three days after they were some 1,000 miles south-east of Monte Video, "and this time we should have an easier chance of finding the victim."

"But what good will that do us?" asked Gilbert; "we want to find the privateer, not the poor vessels it has sunk."

"Have patience, Mr. Romer. A detective seeks for evidence on the spot where a crime is committed before he gives chase, if the thief or murderer has gone out of sight," and Deane switched on the X-rays and set up the screen.

In spite of all the information given, the search seemed hopeless, for during four days of cruising at many depths no result accrued.

On the night of the fifth day the second officer, who had the watch, called the skipper up.

They were lying alongside the sunken "St. George" in 100 fathoms of water.

A huge gap in her side indicated the work of a torpedo, and the great vessel had settled down upon the slime that was by degrees to engulf her.

"See," cried Gilbert, suddenly, "the Boers have fastened their colours to the wreck," and there, on to the stump of a mainsail, was nailed the Vierkleur, the ends being tied to stanchions, so that it was fully disclosed, as if spread to the breezes.

"Then they've certainly been on board. We'll see if they have left any news behind," said Deane, and he called for the diving suits.

Bob, as usual, desired to accompany him, the others, after their recent awful experience, being none too eager to do so, and the two alone were soon climbing over ropes and fallen spars on board the wreck.

But here were sights more awful than they had witnessed before, for it was too sadly evident that quite a number of the crew had not had time to escape.

There they lay—their work done on earth—good men, the bravest of the brave, slain in as dastardly a manner as one who is killed by an assassin from behind.

Ship to ship, man to man, British vessels and British sailors fear no foe; but the sneaking submarine, that can strike unseen, that can destroy without fear of being harmed —that cowardly foe no man, however brave, can resist.

It is on a par with the barbarous poisons of the middle ages, a disgrace to civilisation, a shame to any country.

Sea assassins are the submarines, and the nations who attack with them can no longer be met as honourable foes.

Bob, busy in the flag-room, soon pulled out a Union Jack, and, tearing down the Vierkleur, he fastened the good old British flag in its place, a hearty cheer on board the "Nautilus," from those who were watching at the portholes, greeting this achievement.

Then Deane, holding a box in his hands, beckoned to the boy to leave, and both quickly returned to the "Nautilus."

"Open that box again!" he cried, as soon as his helmet was off, and he sat, panting, on a chest.

Buchan opened it, and pulled out several charts, dripping with water.

"That's it, that's it!" cried Deane, excitedly, pointing to one among them; and then, in answer to the many questions put to him: "It's the Boers' chart. I was sure of it."

"Chart of what? How will it help us?" asked Sir Peter.

"If I'm not mistaken, Sir Peter, it's the chart of their hiding-place, their port."

"But how came it there?" was the question put by doubting Gilbert.

"I can't say, but I should think someone took the chart case on board to put whatever charts he could steal from the 'St. George' into it, not knowing, or forgetting, that their own chart was inside, and then came away in a hurry and left it on board."

"Unless it has been done to deceive us and lead us astray," said Gilbert, with the cautiousness of a lawyer.

"I don't think so, Mr. Romer. It's a carefully-made-out chart, and it's been much used, and by dirty hands, too," and Deane showed where the lines had been thumbed.

"I believe you are right, Deane," said Sir Peter, slowly; "and if you are, you will be a rich man if we live to come back. We'll leave you now to study the chart, and to take us to where the Boers hide."

CHAPTER XI.

WITH the chart, found so providentially, spread upon the cabin table, Sir Peter and his friends turned to Captain Deane to explain it to them.

"The course, Sir Peter, is due south from here," said the skipper. "Here"—and he pointed to a dotted line—"one may expect icebergs, and here ice-floes. This ice would stop any ordinary vessel, but the submarine apparently goes under, for the track is marked, and I feel sure that it does not mean through the floe."

"And what is this?" asked Sir Peter.

"Apparently open sea beyond the floe, and within two hundred and fifty miles of the South Pole. This, Sir Peter, is an island, and here is the harbour."

"But I thought that there was no open sea so far south," said Gilbert.

"No one, unless it is these people, has ever got so far south as to explore. There may be a warm current there from submarine hot springs. This looks as though it were meant for a volcano," and he pointed to a circle of dots on the island.

"But the further you go south the colder it becomes; we know that, don't we?" remarked Sir Peter.

"Neither the North nor the South Poles are the centres of the greatest cold, Sir Peter. No, it's possible for a submarine to get so far," mused the skipper.

"Then, if she can do it, we can," cried Bob, with enthusiasm.

"Right, my lad, for if Boers can do anything, why Britishers can," cried Sir Peter, cheerily. "We seem to have chanced on the key of this mystery; now to see if we can't open the door of captivity."

"And if we meet the Boers, my Mauser is in splendid order," remarked Bob, going to the rifle stand and taking down his favourite weapon.

Down south was now the order, and into the grey seas the "Nautilus" proceeded at half speed. The voyage was monotonous, but Sir Peter got up shooting contests, wrestling matches, and various games to pass the time, and there was no grumbling, only a grim wish of all on board to meet with the Boers again.

Some time was lost by a heavy storm for eight-and-forty hours, as during

"MANAGED TO THROW THE ROPE OVER THE PRIVATEER'S PROPELLER."

No. 3.

most of this time the vessel had to keep beneath the surface.

Once, while floating above for a little while, a four-masted ship was seen, with some of her sails in tatters, running before the gale, probably with wheat from 'Frisco, but it was too rough to speak her.

Another time the "Nautilus" passed through a school of whales, and one old bull determined on charging her; and so, meeting her steel ram, he died the death of the imprudent.

The shock, however, was felt fore and aft, and the sea was red for some way around.

The rest of the school fled, Bob being much interested in noticing how two mothers with baby whales swam behind them so as to guard them from danger.

"I reckon one of them is fine big fish for a net," Bill Yeo remarked; but Bob, with his superior knowledge, answered:

"A whale is not a fish, Bill, but an animal."

"So I should think when I seed one a walking past our front garden," retorted Bill.

"Bill, if you don't know, don't let everyone see how ignorant you are," said Bob, angrily.

"I know a fish when I seed one."

"But I tell you a whale is not a fish, and if I say so, it is so."

The two lads might have quarrelled had not Sir Peter come up at this moment and put matters right, and Bill went below muttering:

"Think I don't know fins and a tail—and me a fisherman!"

"When you correct anyone, Bob, do it better. Don't let it seem that you are the superior. I daresay Bill knows many things you don't."

"Very likely," said Bob, abashed.

"We are all ignorant," said Sir Peter; "we know so few things, and we don't know so many. Now, Bob, let me see how your shooting hand is able to work," and Bob, always eager to fire his Mauser, soon forgot his annoyance.

Small icebergs now came in sight every hour, with here and there huge mountains of ice that had to be skirted.

Sunshine was scarce now, foggy weather being prevalent, and Captain Deane, taking advantage of a spell of sunshine, took an observation, which gave a situation at 51deg. 30min. longitude, and 67deg. 39min. of south latitude.

They soon approached solid fields of ice with but few breaks in them, and the air reservoirs were filled preparatory to taking the long subsea passage under the frozen surface.

The crew were allowed on deck to have a last mouthful of fresh air for a time, for in a couple of hours the hatches were to be closed until the open sea was found south.

"It looks dreadfully dreary," observed Bob to his uncle, as the two stood together looking over the vast grey plains of ice so still and devoid of life. He was thinking of 'Beth—if she were alive and a prisoner, with such an outlook, it would break her once merry little heart.

Gilbert Romer tried to speak, but the words seemed to swell in his throat.

Life seemed as frozen and dismal as the prospect, and hope as far off as summer. He grasped the boy's sympathetic hand, and pressed it, and Bob understood.

"No skating there, Master Bob," observed Bill Yeo. "I thought ice was smooth."

"Not Polar ice, that's always hummacky," replied Bob, with an air of "Ask-me-what-you-like-and-I'll- tell you."

"All below!" called out Captain Deane, and instinctively those on deck drew long breaths of the keen air before descending. All knew that it might be the last time that they would see daylight again; but if one or two felt faint-hearted, they showed no white feather.

At a depth of about nine hundred feet open water was found, and again the "Nautilus" made her way to the south, this time at nearly full speed, for it was necessary to stay under water as short a time as possible in case of an accident.

For thirty-seven hours the monotonous journey continued, the vessel having sometimes to deviate for a while where the bottom shallowed and supported huge icebergs.

Once, even the depths of the sea were agitated as a huge berg turned turtle, and in falling smashed up the smaller ice near, causing waves that sprang from the very bed of the ocean; but as a rule there was only perfect silence around. It was just after this time that the "Nautilus" was suddenly stopped, and then backed, and stopped again.

"What is the matter, Captain?" Sir Peter asked, as the skipper came into the saloon and took out the Boer chart and measured it again very carefully.

"We are following the route marked, sir, as near as I can make it out; but there are big banks along here, and there is ice on them," was the reply.

"So that you can't get under?" enquired Gilbert.

"So that we can't get under, Mr. Romer. Still, if we can't go under we must go round. I shall try west."

Searching ahead with her lights, the "Nautilus" slowly passed westward, the look-outs searching for a passage under the huge glaciers that barred the way to the south. For twelve hours she kept as close to the barrier as she was able to, but no passage could be seen.

Again and again Captain Deane looked at the chart, and each time with a face more anxious.

"Has the ice formed since the chart was made?" asked Sir Peter.

"It's more than ten thousand years old, sir. No, I'm afraid that this was altered from a true chart to mislead us, on the off-chance of our finding it."

"To what purpose?" asked Gilbert.

"I can't say, sir, exactly," answered the skipper, not wishing to let it be understood that it was just possible that, having ventured so far, they could not get out again. "Still," he added, "this chart's been altered, and not made specially. I'm convinced that the retreat is south, and that there is some way there under the ice, only, instead of giving it to us, they've purposely sent us astray. We mustn't go further now, we must try back."

At full speed the "Nautilus" covered the distance in eight hours that had taken her twelve hours to do, and then she slowed again as the Captain began to examine the glacier upon the other side.

"The air's getting very stuffy, Sir Peter," Bob complained.

"It is. Captain Deane, isn't it time it was replenished?"

"We must husband it, Sir Peter," answered Deane. "As soon as possible you shall have fresh, Stir the chemicals, Bob."

They had now been over fifty hours below, but air was stored for one hundred and twenty, if used carefully. Twelve hours' search was to be made towards the east, and then, if unsuccessful, Captain Deane reckoned on having just enough time to get free from the ice fields.

Suddenly the vessel stopped again. The lights through the ports showed, instead of the usual wall, a great black chasm.

"This must be it, Sir Peter. If you look at this chart you will see that the line originally ran to the east, and then was rubbed out and altered. Shall we try?" asked Deane.

"Certainly. Go ahead, and don't lose time. This bad air makes my head ache. Can't we have a little more fresh air."

"Wait a little, Sir Peter. I daren't run risks," and going to the keyboard he touched a button, and, obedient to the order, the "Nautilus" entered the way between the great ice walls.

For several hours the submarine passed through a valley of the width of a large river, but after a time the ice walls narrowed, and they were so close together that they nearly touched the vessel, and then Captain Deane stopped her.

"I daren't go further, Sir Peter. We must give up and get back to the open sea with all speed."

"It's disheartening. How long shall we be doing this?"

"Forty-five hours, Sir Peter. We have air for more, but it won't do to run to the end of it."

Mr. Buchan, the chief engineer, came in at this moment, his face white.

"Captain Deane, a word, please."

The skipper went over to him.

"What's wrong?" he asked.

"The big reserve cylinder has been leaking. We haven't air for twenty-four hours left!"

"Full speed astern! Keep this to yourself, Buchan. Let all who can sleep. Don't let any move more than they can help; they will use less air."

"What is wrong, Captain?" Bob enquired.

"We have to economise air, that's all. So go to sleep, please, all; or if you can't, sit still, and use as little as you can."

"But we have enough, haven't we?" asked Sir Peter.

"I hope so, Sir Peter."

The millionaire looked keenly at the stern face, and said nothing. He knew that a fight for life was a-head.

"Come on; all lie down," he said. "Now, all must obey orders strictly."

Then swiftly the "Nautilus" hurried towards the light, a panting, aching crew on board, praying for a mouthful of keen air, suffocated almost beyond endurance by the heavy atmosphere that was to be theirs for nearly two days longer.

CHAPTER XII.

How slowly the clock seemed to go. Nothing to do but to watch the chronometers, to pant out the minutes, while throbbing heads and burning eyes made each moment an age of pain.

The fresh oxygen was given out in such small quantities that it never appeared to put new life into the heavy air. There was just enough to sustain life, and no more. Several of the crew were seized with nausea, some were almost in a state of coma, but Buchan, strong man as he was, kept at work in the engine-room by himself, and the engines throbbed unceasingly.

Twenty-four hours more before the open sea would be reached, and men were on the verge of madness.

The black cook had threatened to break open the last cylinder of air, which was to keep life in them during the last day, and to use it at once.

Buchan, staggering, and almost blind with pain, kept to his task unrelieved, at his own request, and Captain Deane, in the conning-tower, sat like a statue, steering for dear life.

The "Nautilus" was now like a ship of death, so silent were all; even the cook had not the energy left to threaten.

Sometimes a groan broke the stillness as men here and there unconsciously gave utterance to their feelings.

Six hours more and the "Nautilus" was steered upward, only to find ice above, as Deane had expected.

A few valuable minutes had been lost, and he promised himself that he would not try the surface again until

he was sure that the distance to the open sea had been covered.

Four hours of the six had passed, and Gilbert Romer, turning feebly, saw Bob lying apparently dead, and yet had not the strength to find out.

"Oh! for one breath of air," was the thought of all, and Buchan, red-eyed, whispered hoarsely to the Captain that every cylinder was now empty.

"Try more speed," came the order, faintly.

"She's doing her best," said the engineer, and the two men sat there and watched the dull waters around.

Again the bow of the vessel was directed upward, and again it met with resistance; then once more the "Nautilus" hurried northward.

There was a heavy thud, and Deane glanced at the fallen engineer, who had fainted, and was breathing with heavy labour.

The skipper set his teeth; if he, too, fainted, all would be lost, for there was now no one else capable of steering.

His head was swimming, his eyes hardly saw more than blurred images now; he felt that the end was near.

For the last time he steered for the surface, and again the resistance of the ice repelled the vessel. How much further had they to go?

They should have reached the edge of the floe, but it was ever shifting, and where they were it might be a little broader.

That little would mean death to them; he knew that.

The keys of the steering-board danced before his eyes; he would try to find air once more, and he touched one. Instead of rising, the vessel sank rapidly—he could feel that.

Blindly he touched another key, and the "Nautilus" turned quickly to port.

He fell forward on to the keyboard, and pressed down another key as he fainted. The submarine pointed upward, and from a deeper depth than they had hitherto been travelling at sped to the ice above.

The steel ram crashed into it with terrific force; it happened to be somewhat rotten, and the "Nautilus" crashed through and upward, and then fell back on the ice, breaking it and scattering it around her.

The shock roused Deane.

He saw daylight through the thick glass of the conning-tower, and knew that they had found safety.

With a little whining cry like that of a tired child, he essayed to unscrew the bolt that held the top down. He could not move it, he was so weak.

He kicked Buchan to rouse him, but the engineer did not move.

Again he tried the bolt with frantic strength.

It moved a little, and he staggered back, then flew at it again as though it were an enemy he was grappling with.

It moved more; it was loose; the bar came away in his trembling hands, and with the last remnant of his strength he pushed up the top of the conning-tower and then fell insensible beside Buchan.

The engineer was the first to rouse.

He was very cold, he thought, and his head was very bad.

He looked up; the hatch was up, and the cold air was coming in freely.

He staggered to his feet, and then threw open all doors, and the fresh air came sweet and strong to those who had thought that they would never again breathe it.

In two hours a dozen of the strongest men were able to move about, and in two days all had more or less recovered, the "Nautilus" remaining where she had found daylight.

Then at last came the order to get under weigh, and the vessel had to be cut free from the ice which now held her. The cylinders were filled, and the vessel was sunk and headed for the north.

In two hours open water was found, and danger was over, but weary-looking faces told how keen had been the suffering of the past.

"And now what do you propose doing?" asked Sir Peter of the skipper.

"Have you had enough of danger?" asked Deane.

"Have you, Captain?"

"No, Sir Peter."

"Has any man on board?"

"I'll muster them and ask," and soon crew and passengers were assembled on deck.

"Officers and men," said Captain Deane, "we have passed through great danger and great suffering."

"Awful, capen," said the cook, and there was a sympathetic sigh of approval at this rejoinder.

"The Boers have got the better of us, so far. Shall we give up the chase and acknowledge ourselves beaten, or shall we risk more in the hope of rescuing those in peril, avenging our countrymen, and freeing our seas from a great danger?"

Buchan stepped forward, his strong face set determinedly.

"Captain Deane," he said, "speaking for myself, I would never give up the chase, and I don't think any man here is so un-British as to acknowledge himself beaten."

There was a rousing cheer at these words, and if any man had desired to retreat, he was ashamed to say so.

One and all agreed to continue the chase.

"Only mend dat der cylinder," said the cook.

"It is done. We will not remain under so long this time. I propose to wait about here until the privateer comes along. I am convinced that she must pass very near, either coming out or going into her retreat, and once we find her again she sha'n't shake us off," said Deane.

"And thank you all, friends, for your determination to stand by us," cried Sir Peter. "You sha'n't lose by it."

Three weeks were now spent cruising up and down at the edge of the ice fields, and then one morning came the news that the privateer, well out of water, was in sight.

Surely enough she was coming at half speed, those on board never dreaming that their enemy was so nigh.

The conning-tower of the "Nautilus" was so covered with ice that, as it lay just above water, it looked merely like the rest of the ice about, and the privateer passed without making a discovery of it, going westward.

Captain Deane at once followed, and crept very near, going under water now, and using the screen to show the position of the chase.

A few hours afterwards the privateer went under the floe almost at the exact spot where the "Nautilus" had first gone under, and headed due south.

For nearly two days the course was kept, for they were not going as fast as when the "Nautilus" had entered by herself, and then, after a little search, the privateer entered the very same crevasse that the "Nautilus" had done.

"Why, we've tried this before. Is this another slim dodge? Be careful, Deane," said Sir Peter.

"I think we're all right. If she goes to the point where we couldn't turn she can't get away, for we shall block the road. Besides, I don't think the Boers know they are being followed."

Of a sudden the Boer vessel dived and disappeared, the screen no longer showing her picture.

Deane stopped the "Nautilus," for she had gone on some fathoms, and halted as nearly as possible at the spot where the privateer had sunk, and then dropped his vessel carefully.

A close examination showed a strong current coming through a tunnel at right angles, at a depth of about two hundred and seventy feet, and into this tunnel Deane steered.

"Full speed ahead!" was now the order, for the current was strong, and only slow progress was made; but the channel gradually widened, and then opened so that the sides could not be seen.

The water was evidently warm, for the temperature on board the "Nautilus" rose nearly ten degrees, and Deane tried the surface and found it free from ice.

The "Nautilus" was floating in a wide sea, with but little ice about, and a mile a-head was the privateer.

On the horizon was a dim coast-line, and the sky was red at one point.

"That's the volcano, Sir Peter," the captain said, pointing it out, "and, according to the chart, that's the place we want."

CHAPTER XIII.

THE Boer privateer was making straight for the north of the island, which was about thirty miles away.

The "Nautilus" closed upon her until within half a mile, still apparently unseen by the Boers.

As they approached the island dense forests of fir could be seen inland toward the volcano, and precipitous cliffs towered as far as could be viewed, without a break, save where a river cut the rock.

The stream from this river ran right out to sea, and was evidently the cause of the warmth.

Apparently it came directly from the volcano, which every half-hour or so flared up.

As the "Nautilus" neared the shore within a couple of miles, the heat became oppressive, but the privateer kept steadily on, and still the British submarine followed.

"What do you propose to do, Deane?" asked Sir Peter, who had called a council of war in the saloon.

"I propose to follow the privateer to ascertain where she goes. If unobserved, to stay near her under water until sleeping-time, and then to try and capture her."

"And if we are discovered?" asked Gilbert.

"Then, Mr. Romer, we shall have to find out all we can about the place, and keep away, and find some means of communicating with the prisoners."

"We have plenty of arms and ammunition on board," observed Sir Peter. "I have hopes of being able to arm our friends; but I quite see the force of capturing the privateer. If we are in possession of it, the Boers are prisoners on the island, and may come to terms with us."

"Now that we have tracked the vessel home, would it not be better to destroy her?" suggested Gilbert.

"No, Mr. Romer; I think not," said Deane. "We might have an accident with one vessel, for it's awkward navigation hereabouts, and it's no use throwing away the second string to our bow."

"Yes. You're right. We couldn't live here for ever with the Boers."

Yet Gilbert, as he spoke, thought that if he were alone with Marjory, they could make a paradise of the wilderness.

"Live here? What, without theatres and streets? I should think not," cried Bob, whose practical nature had little romance in it.

Bang!

All in the saloon sprang to their feet, when another bang and a thud sent them falling like nine-pins. In a second Captain Deane was at the keyboard, and instantly the "Nautilus" sank, but not before another shell had burst close by, the water dashing against the ports.

"They're firing from the cliffs," called out Bill Yeo, who was in the conning-tower, with instructions to follow the privateer.

"Are we hit?" asked Sir Peter, anxiously.

Mr. Buchan came in hurriedly.

"We've been struck by a shell, or a piece of one, and some of the rivets forward are started," he said.

"Leaking?" asked Deane.

"Very little. Nothing to harm, but they've got our distance."

"Keep her pumped out, Mr. Buchan, and caulk if you can, or cover with plates. We'll get into some place where we can repair, if it's not a long job."

"Forty-eight hours, I should say, if no plate is cracked."

"I am afraid that the privateer was aware that we were following, and enticed us under the fire of a battery on the cliffs.

"The shell must have struck us obliquely, as we were end on, and I think with Buchan, that no harm is done, but we must seek another landing-place."

"They'll make it hot for us when we land, eh?" said Gilbert.

"This is evidently a large island, Mr. Romer, and a few Boers can't be in possession of the whole of it. We'll keep out of sight, and work round to the south side," said Deane.

The "Nautilus" rose cautiously a couple of miles away, and Deane reported that the privateer had gone up the river, and that a flag-staff was to be seen bearing the Verkeleur flag on the heights above it.

"The camp must be near there," he said, "and if we go to the south, we shall have the mountain between us."

Twenty miles or so along the coast the "Nautilus" stopped before a creek, and, entering carefully, found that it wound between high walls of granite.

There was a shelving beach, just the place for repairs, and the cliff here was so overhanging that if any Boers peered down they could see nothing nor find a mark for a shot.

Then, too, they were nearer the captives than if the vessel had gone south, and so she was beached, and in two days the necessary repairs were made by Buchan and his men.

Then came the question how to reach the top of the cliffs and reconnoitre toward the Boers' camp. It seemed impossible to all but the sanguine Bob and his faithful follower, Bill Yeo.

"I've climbed 'em near as bad in Cornwall, Master Bob," said the lad.

"I can see a way just under the ledge right along. If we can reach it, and I know I can, we can find a way."

It was dangerous work, but it must be tried everyone agreed, and the two boys were light and active. A ball of twine was placed in Bill's pocket, with instructions to lower the end if they reached the top, and with that to draw up a rope, which in turn would bring up a rope ladder.

It was impossible to climb straight up, the overhanging summit forbade that, and Bob fancied that he could see a way, about half the distance up, that could be taken along the face of the cliffs to a spot where it would be easier to reach the top.

Up to this way it was pretty easy climbing, and the two lads reached a spot where they sat down for a rest, panting with their exertions.

Below, their friends looked the size of shilling dolls; above, the granite seemed to be threatening to fall at once.

"'Taint more nor I've of'en done after nests," said Bill, as he dangled his legs over a depth of some three hundred feet.

"This is the easiest part, Bill; we've the worst before us," remarked Bob, gravely.

His boyish exuberance had sobered down now that he knew how much depended upon him.

"I'm ready, Master Bob, to go on," said Bill; "and wouldn't I just like to drop a stone on cook's head afore we left here. It 'ud make him stare, and I could just reach 'im."

"There's no time for fooling. Let's get on—I'll lead," and Bob crept along the face of the cliff, stepping from one jutting crag to another, sometimes pressing flat against the side, sometimes able to move freely, until at last the way was stopped by a smooth wall without a ledge for thirty feet above or below.

"We shall have to go back and try another path, Bill," said Bob, after a survey of the surroundings.

"Back it is, sir," cried Bill, cheerily, and led the way for fifty yards, until a huge jutting mass of rock stopped the path.

"This isn't the way we came, Bill," said Bob.

Bill looked dolefully around.

"That 'taint, and I can't quite make out which is," he said.

On all sides the cliff seemed smooth and pathless, and there was now no going backwards or forwards.

"Something's got to be done," said Bob, after a pause.

"There's a path a goodish bit below," said Bill, craning over, "and I think if we could get to it, it leads right up to that slope, and we could easy get up there to the top."

"Yes, but how are we going to get to that path? It's fifty feet below us."

"We can't both do it, Master Bob, but one of us could let t'other down."

"What, with that string? It won't bear us, and, besides, what is the other to do?"

"T'other must wait here until a ladder is let down from the top. The string I can plait, and that'll be strong enough."

"I suppose we must risk it. You'll have to let me down carefully."

"You are the strongest, Master Bob, and I'm the lightest."

"Which means that I've got to stop here. Well, I suppose I must let you go," grumbled Bob, taking the string and giving it to Bill.

For an hour the sailor boy's nimble fingers were busy, and at the end of the time a fairly strong line of sixty feet was ready, and the end being hitched round a boulder, Bill put his foot in a loop, and Bob began to lower him gently.

One slip, once let the line run from his sore hands, torn with the knots, and Bob knew that his companion would be dashed to atoms far below, while his fate might be even worse, and so, bracing against the strain, he held on until he heard Bill's welcome cry:

"All safe, Master Bob; let down the line."

Then Bob let it down, and watched Bill climb slowly along until he reached the slope he had spoken of, when he soon disappeared behind a huge mass of rock.

"Those boys are a long time gone," said Gilbert Romer, some three hours after this. "I hope nothing has happened to them. I ought to have gone."

"They were best fitted to take the risk," said Sir Peter. "We must wait and hope."

"Hallo! what's this?" cried

Buchan, as he pointed to a stone suspended far above their heads, and apparently sailing down towards them like a feather, the string which held it not being visible so far off.

Down it came, attached to a frayed line of knotted strings, for Bill had been obliged to unplait his rope and tie up the bits.

A stronger line was attached to the string, and anxiously those below watched it go up, fearing every minute that the string would break. Then a stone was thrown down, and it was taken as a signal that a stronger rope might be attached, and this, in time, was up, and made fast,

but some way along the cliffs, and up this one of the most active of the men climbed.

Then a rope ladder was lowered and made fast, until a fairly safe means of reaching the top was made, and another line was then let down to Bob so that he was released from his perilous position.

"First-rate, boys," said Sir Peter, when, after a hard struggle, he reached the summit up the turning, swaying ladder. "You've made everything possible for us now. We must pull up the guns and ammunition, and a good supply of provisions, leave a guard on the 'Nautilus,' and then reconnoitre."

CHAPTER XIV.

WHILE some hauled up the guns and other requirements, the rest of the party began to build a fort, which would command all the ground near, and serve them if pressed at any time.

It was well provisioned, and a pom-pom was soon peeping from an embrasure in it. Water could be drawn up from the river beneath, and Sir Peter reckoned that their force could stand a siege of six months if necessary.

A number of bushes and stunted trees around were cut down, and a few boulders were moved up to the fort to strengthen the walls, leaving a bare expanse in front of the fort which no force would dare to cross.

"Sha'n't we have wire entanglements?" asked Bob, who was well read in the history of the war at the Cape.

"Not necessary, Bob," said his uncle, "but we might have a line or two hung with bells, so as to give us an alarm if the enemy blundered against them in the dark."

"I think not, Mr. Romer," remarked Sir Peter; "we must trust to our sentries. If the bells are put up, they are apt to be rung by some fox or other animal, and then away goes ammunition, and we alarm any Boers in the neighbourhood."

"I agree with Sir Peter," said Captain Deane. "Sailors are used to

look-out, and there's nothing like a good sentry."

"To be shot at," said Gilbert, drily.

"Yes, sometimes," said Sir Peter. "In South Africa hundreds of sentries have been stalked and shot by Boers, but we'll build three sangars, and let them watch from there."

"What, stone forts?" asked Bob.

"Yes, they are quickly made. I want to start on our reconnoitre as soon as possible. We shall have no night here for a long time yet, but there is a twilight for a couple of hours."

"May I go with you?" pleaded Bob.

"I suppose that nothing can go on without your wanting a finger in the pie, young man?"

"Nothing, Sir Peter," said Bob, promptly, at which speech all laughed.

"Very well, then. I propose to take Buchan, Captain Deane, and to leave you in charge here."

"As you will, Sir Peter," said the sturdy seaman, his voice showing keen disappointment. The love of adventure had not yet been quenched in him, despite his many years at sea.

"I hope I may come," said Gilbert.

"Certainly; I counted on your help, and I think that the lad Yeo might be useful. He and Bob seem to work well together."

"Bill's a good lad, and does what he's told," remarked Bob, with an air of grave condescension.

"That's right; and now we want Bob to be a good lad and to do what he's told, and only what he's told," said Sir Peter, with a smile.

"Am I to wait until you're shot, and then to ask your permission to fire?" Bob asked slyly.

"You obey orders at all hazards, even at the risk of our lives. Disobedience may sometimes do good, but nine times out of ten it does harm."

"Nelson disobeyed," argued Bob.

"But you're not Nelson, my boy. Nelson was above all rules because he was cleverer than those in command."

Bob grinned.

"Haven't had my chance yet, Sir Peter," and then he ran off to tell Bill Yeo of his good fortune.

Carrying two days' provisions with them, the small party of five marched quietly away, Gilbert a couple of hundred yards in front scouting.

All were well armed with Mausers and revolvers, and prepared to risk life and liberty on behalf of the captives.

The distance to the camp of the Boers could not be estimated, but Gilbert put it down at thirty miles over rocky ground.

The bush, mostly of mimosa, was dense, though stunted, with sometimes woods of firs, and occasionally the volcano would spurt fire and light up the sky with carmine, which faded to orange, and subsided in the deepest blue.

Despite the rockiness of the ground, there were no great obstacles to surmount, and the going was fairly easy, although had a Boer force been there to meet them, it would have been impossible for the Britishers to have gone a quarter of a mile, for with such cover every one of them could have been shot down without a foe showing himself.

But the Boers were happy in a belief that their gun had sunk the "Nautilus," and they felt so secure in their retreat that they never believed for a moment that any force would dare to approach their camp, if indeed such a force could land, which they imagined was impossible.

In eight hours about eighteen miles had been covered, and there were no signs of the camp. Sir Peter, who had been used to travelling across vast tracks of wild land, acted as guide, and he took his bearings by the volcano, which a few miles away loomed up black toward the sky.

A camp was now formed, and a few boulders made a wall, behind which all but Gilbert slept, he taking the first watch.

How wonderful and how dreadful it all seemed. Here, cut off from civilisation, perhaps for ever, were he and—he hoped—the girl who had promised to be his wife.

Neither of them had quarrelled with any man, and yet man had separated them so that their suffering was almost beyond bearing.

He, a strong man, could perhaps live through it; but how could she, a girl brought up with kindness and amidst comfort?

He longed to tell her how near he was, to bid her hope, to speak one word of love to her.

Slowly passed the hours, and Buchan took second watch, but Gilbert did not sleep, but watched with him.

Sir Peter took the third watch, for the time of rest—there being no night it could only be so called—was divided into three watches only, so that the lads should not be called upon to give up any portion of much-needed sleep.

Then came breakfast, without a fire, for it was impossible to light one when it might warn the enemy, and then the journey was continued.

Once they had to march almost along the cliff bordering the sea, and here were countless thousands of gulls of all sorts, which rose screaming until Gilbert feared that their alarm might warn the Boers.

Sir Peter, however, thought that as the enemy was not expecting them, they would take no heed of this.

Yet, as soon as possible, they left the nesting-grounds, and continued the journey inland.

Gilbert was still in advance, but as they passed a huge boulder, smooth with age, Bob made Bill Yeo give him a leg up so that he was able to reach the top, some forty feet high.

"I can see them," he cried, a moment after. "I can see houses, and a man with a rifle."

Buchan helped Sir Peter up, and he, using his glasses, saw plainly the camp with over eighty huts in it.

A council of war was held at the foot of the boulder, and then Sir Peter told the two boys to creep forward, and without being seen, find out, if possible, what the road was like, and how it was guarded, if at all.

He made them leave their rifles behind them, in case they might be tempted to use them, and so give the alarm, much to Bob's annoyance.

In an hour they returned breathless.

"It's a plain track," panted Bob. "You can do it in half an hour, and there's only one man to be seen doing sentry duty."

"How far from the camp is he?" asked Sir Peter.

"A quarter of a mile, but there are six big huts near him where I think the prisoners are, and he's sentry over them," explained Bob.

"Very likely. I don't think they expect us. We must get hold of that sentry, and squeeze all the information out of him as to their strength and position."

"Shall I shoot him so that he won't be killed?" asked Bob, eagerly. "I can easily."

"Yes, and rouse the camp. No, I came prepared for this," said Sir Peter, as he took from his pack a long strip of untanned leather, on which was an iron ring.

"Is it a lasso?" Gilbert asked.

"Yes. I've used it in South America when I was younger," Sir Peter explained, "and I think I am still smart enough to capture a stupid Boer."

He slung it carefully over his left arm so that the ring with the loop would run easily, and then the little party crept forward until a silent warning from Bob told them that at the next turn of the path the sentry would be seen.

From this point Sir Peter stole forward by himself, and they saw him balancing the leather coils ready for swinging the lasso forward.

First he peeped round, and then crept forward.

They heard the whizz of the lasso, and a heavy thud told them that the sentry had been thrown down, and all ran forward, to find Sir Peter sitting on the Boer's chest as he lay there, dazed by his fall, while with skilful hands Sir Peter gagged him.

CHAPTER XV.

Bob and Bill Yeo exhibited signs of great delight on seeing the bulky form of the Boer stretched on the ground.

The man was strongly secured, and as he came to, a pistol held against his head was an argument for silence that he quite understood.

He looked from one to another of the group beside him with wonderment, but his little eyes gleamed viciously.

"Now, understand me," said Sir Peter, sternly, to the prisoner. "Answer my questions promptly, or I shall shoot you. Don't pretend you don't understand English, and

don't tell lies, for I know a good bit already, and I shall test you; and if you lie to me, you'll speak no more. Understand?"

"Ach! Verdomte bergschatten (This is a bad business)!" growled the Boer.

"Your name?" asked the baronet.

"Henrich Vaugan."

"How many men are here?"

"Twenty tousand."

"Think again."

And Sir Peter pressed the muzzle of the revolver against the man's forehead.

"You daren't shoot me. I am a

prisoner of war," said the Boer, sulkily, scowling at his captor.

"I give you my word I shall shoot you without remorse, my friend," Sir Peter answered. "I'm not a fool fresh from England. I've lived in Johannesburg for over ten years."

The Boer looked keenly at him.

"I thought I knew you," he said. "I was a zarp there. I wish I'd never left. I'd have served your countrymen faithfully."

"Don't ask me to believe you. Now that you know I'm a Transvaal man, lately an Outlander, you'll understand that I know you, and that I won't stand nonsense. How many men have you here?"

"Seven hundred," was the sulky reply.

"Tell me to a man; you're not right yet."

"Five hundred and twenty-seven."

"How many fighting men?"

"All."

"Think again."

And again the pistol pressed against the prisoner's forehead.

"Four hundred are goot, I tell you. The others we put in front."

"And force them to fight?" said Sir Peter, cheerily. "I understand your methods. How many prisoners have you?"

"Eight hundred and forty. I don't know to twenty."

"That will do. How many of these are ladies?"

"Only seven."

"Are the Miss Grants quite safe?"

"Oh, dere safe enough," the man said, with a grin.

Gilbert and Bob exchanged glances. How thankful they were no words could tell.

"You thought you were safe just now. How many sentries are there, and where are they posted?"

No reply.

The millionaire put the muzzle of the pistol before the Boer's eyes.

"I'll count three. One—two——"

"There's four sentries over the prisoners; dat's all," said the prisoner, hurriedly, anxious to speak before it was too late.

"Ah! You're sensible, but don't try my temper," said Sir Peter. "Now, what is the watchword?"

"Kruger," growled the Boer.

"Thanks. That is all we require for the present. Now, my friend, we'll gag you for a little. My friend here is going to the village on the strength of your password. If he doesn't return within six hours I shall think you have told us wrong, and I shall shoot you. It is now a quarter to three. Say, at nine o'clock."

"I haf forgot. It was Majuba, not Kruger," said the Boer.

"We'll try Majuba, then," said Sir Peter, who then proceeded to gag the prisoner and to tie him up.

"Mr. Romer," said the millionaire, "I suppose you wish to communicate with your friends?"

"At all risks," cried Gilbert, eagerly.

"We must strip this man, and you must wear his clothes. Not a nice job, as you see; but you must be as like a zarp as you can. As you don't know the Taal, don't speak if you are spoken to. Give the password, then scowl and growl something indefinite and guttural, as though you were in a bad temper and wouldn't talk."

"I'll do it, Sir Peter."

"Take Bob with you."

"Oh, thank you, Sir Peter. That's just what I wanted," cried the delighted lad.

"Disarm him," said the baronet, laughingly, "and take him as your prisoner."

"Oh, I say! Not even my Mauser?" cried Bob.

"No, my lad. You must pretend to be a prisoner, and you must act your part well. Your uncle will take you to where the prisoners are; he will put you with them, and you must tell them we are here, and see how many can escape and join us. Be careful whom you tell; we want only good men."

"I'll do it, Sir Peter," cried Bob, eagerly.

"Very well. Much depends on you. If they can escape, you must lead them to our fortress."

"Bob will do it well, Sir Peter," said Gilbert.

"I'm sure of it. And now to disguise yourself. Plaster your face, hair, and hands with dirt. It will not only disguise your features, but make you look more like a Boer."

Mr. Henrich Vaugan had to part with a considerable quantity of his not very clean costume, a blanket being wrapped around him instead; and soon Gilbert would have passed very well for one of the grand army of De Wet and Company.

After much hand-shaking and many good wishes he and Bob left, Gilbert carrying the Boer's rifle on his left arm, and holding Bob by the collar of his coat with the other hand.

"That must be one of the prisoners' huts," Gilbert said, as they came near to the village after a couple of hours' walk. "Now, Bob, don't forget you are a prisoner."

They came in sight of a sentry, who was sitting down with his Mauser between his knees, smoking.

Gilbert shook Bob, who cried out:

"Please don't shoot me. I won't escape again—indeed, sir, I won't."

"What? Did he get out? Ach! There are so many, I had forgotten him," the sentry cried in the Taal; but Gilbert, not understanding, merely growled out "Majuba," and shook Bob again.

"Oh, sir, don't hurt me—please don't!" cried the lad, and the sentry, rising leisurely, went to the hut, and, taking a key from his pocket, opened the door, when Gilbert thrust Bob in, upon which the door was locked again.

The hut was long and narrow, made of timber, the crevices being filled with moss.

It was badly lighted and reeked; and Bob saw that it was crowded with men.

"What, have they captured more prisoners?" asked a voice in gentlemanly accents, that Bob thought he remembered.

He went closer, and looked at the speaker.

It was the captain of the lost warship, the "St. George."

"Captain Ballance, don't you remember me?" he asked.

"Why, yes. You were on the submarine. Have they sunk her?"

"No, sir. She is here, the Boers don't know where. And my uncle, disguised as a Boer, has pretended that I am his prisoner, and put me here to speak to you."

The men there, sixty or seventy, crowded round on hearing these words, and Bob, in low tones told his tale, with its adventures and dangers.

"Hope at last!" said Captain Ballance. "Now, gentlemen and men all, don't get excited. We may turn the tables on these brutes, if we are careful; but if we make a false move we shall be shot without a moment's warning."

"How's 'Beth?" asked Bob, nervously, blushing like a girl.

"If she is one of the ladies, I believe they are well," answered Captain Ballance.

"I know her, you know," explained Bob. "It was because we found her pigeon, you remember, that we got the submarine and came out here."

"Thank Heaven for 'Beth!" said another of the prisoners; and then, in a whisper, "and the youngster."

"Now, gentlemen and men, we must act quickly, lest anything be found out. We must overpower the sentry when our supper is brought, and make a quick bolt of it. Scatter well at leaving. I'll take the first sentry," said Captain Ballance. "You, Mr. Johnson, must go for the next. Take stones, all of you, and throw them. It will at least put them off their guard. Those that capture the rifles must remain and cover the retreat, and Mr.——"

"Bob Romer," said the youngster.

"And Mr. Bob Romer," continued the captain, "will lead the way at the double until you find shelter."

"We're ready, sir,"

"Anything to get out of this."

"We'll get our own back."

These, with many other such sentences, were the answers from the excited men.

"Supper is due here in half-an-hour. Now get the stones and be ready."

The floor of the hut was the rough, stony ground, and stones were plentiful.

Bob armed himself with a few, and

stood facing the door, waiting for it to open.

There was no speech now; only a stern silence.

The prisoners had been cooped in the hut for weeks, some for months, even when the Boers need have had no fear of their escaping had they given them liberty.

Slowly the minutes died, and then came the tramp of feet

"They are bringing supper—be ready. Don't hit our men who are carrying the dishes. Go for the sentry," said Captain Ballance. "'Tention!"

Bob stood, eager for the start, his right arm thrown well back, as the noise of the key in the lock was heard.

The sentry was talking to the prisoners who were carrying the food.

"Waste of good food, feeding the verdomte rooineks. I'd sink the lot of you!" he growled.

Bob felt the sharp edges of the flint in his hand, and was glad that it was so sharp.

"May it poison dem!" cried the Boer, and threw open the door.

Then, as he stepped aside, Bob's flint struck him between the eyes, and he threw up his hands to his face.

In a moment Captain Ballance had hurled him down, and obtained possession of his rifle, as the three other sentries came forward, wondering what was the matter.

As they did so, they met a shower of stones, at which one fell, the other two firing into the advancing prisoners.

Three prisoners fell wounded, and then the sentries, borne down by numbers, had their rifles and ammunition snatched from them.

Then, headed by Bob, a quick retreat was made, while from the distance a few Boers were to be seen hurriedly approaching.

CHAPTER XVI.

GILBERT ROMER, on leaving Bob a prisoner—not without some qualms of fear for the brave lad—strolled towards the Boer village, which was composed of about one hundred and twenty huts of all sizes.

He wished to find out where the women prisoners were confined, and so he passed on by groups of men who scarcely looked at him, until he came to a house which seemed neater and cleaner than the rest.

There was a little garden round it, planted with a few flowers, white, yellow, and blue, the names of which he did not know.

It struck him that English girls must have done this, and he lounged round to the back.

A girl was stooping over some flowers with her back towards him, but his heart stood still for a moment.

He knew whom it was in an instant.

"Margery!" he called softly.

She stood up and looked round with an air of fear, but her eyes did not rest on him for a second.

She was looking for someone of different appearance.

"Margery, dearest!" he called again.

"Gilbert! Gilbert!" she answered, running to him.

He clasped her to his arms, and for a moment neither could speak.

"How did you come here, dear one? Are you a prisoner? They will shoot you if you are caught near here," she whispered.

"I came to save you. Are all well?"

"Yes. We have all been ill, and that it why we are allowed some liberty. But I am fearful for you."

"I have plenty of good comrades, dear one," he said, anxious to cheer her. "I felt that I must see you, and now I shall be able to return to them with the knowledge that you are safe."

"Now go—go, dear one!" she cried. "Go; there is shooting, and see—the Boers are coming this way."

And as she spoke a crowd of Boers, some loading their rifles as they ran, came from out of the village.

"Come on," they called to Gilbert. "The rooineks have escaped. Come and shoot them down."

He understood their signs, although not their words, and hastily whispering a good-bye to Margery, he ran towards them, hoping to find an opportunity to escape later on.

There was heavy firing to the east now, and soon two men carrying a wounded Boer passed, then another pair, and then another.

Evidently the Britishers were shooting straight.

He joined the fighting line, where men were creeping forward, apparently shooting at empty rocks a thousand yards away.

Two Boers lay on the ground beside him under shelter of the rock, and therefore to keep up the pretence, he fired, but in the air.

One of them noticed it and swore at him, and then the other, in a tone of authority, asked him a question, to which of course he could give no answer.

Then suddenly one sprang on his back, and the other seized his rifle, shouting to others near

He heard them cry out something about the rooinek, and guessed it referred to him.

His arms were bound, and he was marched back, a bullet whizzing uncomfortably close, sent by his friends in the distance, who evidently took him and his captors alike for Boers.

Once out of range, a huge Boer, rather rougher and more unkempt than the others, spoke to him.

"So," he said in English, "we have a spy here. You know how we serve a spy?"

"I came with a message to a lady," Gilbert answered boldly.

"You lie!" snarled the big brute, striking Gilbert with the back of his hand across the mouth so that the blood spurted out.

"You lie, dog! You came to release our prisoners and to spy on us. As soon as we have done our work of killing off those fools yonder, we'll make a target of you. It's dull here, and I'll give a prize for fancy shooting, and you shall be the target. Lock him up," he added to the men near.

And so, a few minutes later, Gil-bert was thrown, still bound, into an evil-smelling and dark hut, to wonder whether hope had come to him only to ny away a moment after and to leave him helpless.

Meantime, the escaped prisoners were making the best of their way to the "Nautilus'" camp, headed by Bob, their retreat covered by Captain Ballance and three of his men, all of whom were expert shots.

Firing, two at a time, the other two retiring, they kept off the Boers who at first took up the pursuit, killing three and wounding several as they advanced, thinking themselves able to rush so few as those of the British who had rifles.

The enemy were now advancing in Zulu style, their front taking the form of a crescent, the ends of which they pressed forward in an endeavour to surround the little party.

It was from one of these wings that Johnson, late chief petty officer of H.M.S. "St. George," fell, shot through the head, as he was retreating to take up a fresh position.

Captain Ballance rushed for the fallen Mauser, so precious to them now, and took possession of the dead man's bandolier; but in retreating he was twice wounded in the arm and head.

Two others of the late prisoners rushed out and got him into safety, and, taking up the two rifles, opened a steady fire on the triumphant Boers, who were now advancing boldly.

A couple of men fell and the rest of the enemy took shelter again, giving the brave defenders a chance to gain a couple of hundred yards to the rear.

A mile behind them was the narrow pass which the rest of the British had now reached.

If the four armed sailors could once reach it they were sure that they could keep the foe at bay until relief was sent from the "Nautilus."

On one side was a high, precipitous wall of rock, below was a depth of two hundred feet, too steep for climbing; and the path was so narrow that only one man could pass along it, save at a few points.

Still firing in pairs, and retreating in pairs, the four men had almost

"'BACK MEN!' SHOUTED CAPTAIN BALLANCE.

reached the pass, when the petty officer, Simons, who had taken command, fell, shot through the thigh.

He rose after he had fallen, and tried to walk, but fell again; and a roar of triumph rose from the Boer ranks, and several of the enemy were seen racing to capture the brave fellow and to secure his rifle.

"Get back, lads," he cried. "You must reach the pass."

And, obedient to command, they raced back, meeting Bob on the way.

Sir Peter and Buchan had been found waiting in the pass, and to them Bob handed over the party; and, borrowing from Buchan his Mauser and cartridges, he was just running to the front when he saw poor Simons fall and his opponents come forward boldly to capture him.

Leaning over a large boulder, and steadying his rifle on it, he aimed for the foremost of the enemy, and had the satisfaction of seeing him fall.

Quickly reloading, he fired again, and brought down his man, his practice on board ship now serving him in good stead.

The rest of the Boers dropped amongst the boulders for security, and Bob, taking advantage of their momentary confusion, ran forward and threw himself down beside Simons.

A couple of bullets struck the ground close beside him, but the Boers had been too flurried to aim well.

"Get back, my lad, this is too exposed," said Simons. "You're only tempting Providence."

"I'm going to bind up your wound. You'll bleed to death else," said Bob, coolly tearing a handkerchief into strips.

"You're a plucky young gentleman," said the petty officer, and passed the end of the handkerchief under his leg, so that Bob could make a bandage, and, using a knife as a tourniquet, did much towards stopping the flow of blood.

"I can't carry you back," he said, "but I'm going to wait here and keep the beggars off."

"Keep behind me, then," urged the sailor.

But Bob refused the rampart, and seeing a head a few hundred yards off, fired at it.

The other three armed Britishers at the head of the pass were now in position, and although Bob did not dare to raise himself, the Boers were checked by their fire, and did not advance.

CHAPTER XVII.

Bob took advantage of the slackness of the Boer firing to roll a few stones in front of himself and his charge, and presently some of the enemy could be seen going back to their camp, apparently for reinforcements.

A couple of sailors at this moment made a dash forward, and, although one was slightly wounded in the attempt, they managed to bring their wounded comrade into the safety of the pass, Bob covering the retreat.

Some of the enemy's bullets came very near to him, one dashing up a fragment of stone that cut his cheek; but beyond this slight wound the lad was untouched.

Before bedtime the entire party had arrived at the little fort on the cliffs above where the "Nautilus" was lying, the wounded men being lowered into the submarine and placed under the care of the cook, with the exception of Captain Ballance, who begged to be allowed to remain in command of his men.

The fort was at once rebuilt on a larger scale, with two strong sangars 1000 yards in advance on either side, each of which was to be held by six men under a petty officer.

The late prisoners were armed, and the jolly sailors worked with a will in getting everything ready for an expected assault.

"But not a thousand men could take this place now, Captain Ballance," Sir Peter said, as he saw the thick ramparts of stones rising.

"They have a couple of biggish

guns, including a 4.7 taken from my poor ship," answered Captain Ballance. "They won't assault us; they'll knock us to pieces."

"Then why waste time in building this? Why not attack them?"

"I am going to remain here in command, Sir Peter, and we shall take a lot of moving yet. Then, while they think they have us all here, I propose that you take half of my men, with Lieutenant Watkins in command, and as many of yours as you can spare, in your 'Nautilus,' round to the Boer encampment. You will be able to release the rest of the prisoners, while the bulk of the fighting men will be occupied here."

"An excellent plan, sir. The only trouble is that we may have to encounter their submarine, and there will be trouble. We don't want to sink her, we shall need her services, and if she sinks us, or both are disabled, we may never get away from this land."

"Could you disable the privateer temporarily?" asked the sailor. "A chain foul of her screw would do it."

"I can do that, Captain Ballance," cried Bob, eagerly. "Bill Yeo and I can put on our diving-suits, and if we are placed anywhere near we'll reach her. She is lying in shallow water—at least, your men say it's all shallow up that creek."

"It will want stronger men than you, young man," said Captain Ballance, smilingly. "Still, I like your spirit, and I hope Sir Peter will allow you to accompany the party. I think you will be able to manage the job. You can creep close up, and let your divers do their work; then run past the privateer and land your company, release the prisoners, and hold the encampment."

"It is to be done, and we'll try," said Sir Peter gravely, "and if you'll tell off those men who are to accompany us, we'll be off. From what I know of the Boers, they'll take their night's rest and advance on you in the morning, and then will be our time."

"And as soon as you have taken the camp, Mr. Watkins," said the captain, addressing his lieutenant, "push on and take the Boers in rear.

You may be in time to get that gun before we're done for."

"We'll lose no time, Captain Ballance," was the prompt reply, and a moment after, at the word of command, the bluejackets mustered, sixty-one in all.

Of these, thirty-one were left to man the forts, supplemented by ten of the "Nautilus" men, six of whom had been in the Navy, and who fell into line naturally enough.

The rest were lowered down the cliffs, and by midnight all were on board the "Nautilus," and the vessel had started away.

*　　*　　*　　*

Margery and her sister were talking sadly together, for Gilbert's capture made them fear the worst for him, when the Boer leader, Van Leer, entered.

He had for a long time past expressed great admiration for Margery, and had tried hard to persuade her to marry him.

As Commandant on the island, he had great power, and he had used it to make the girl's imprisonment harder in his endeavour to force her into marriage, until Margery had fallen ill, and he was compelled to give her some indulgence.

A great, heavy, dull-looking animal of a man; yet he was extremely cunning, and as ferocious as a leader of desperate men is bound to be.

"I haf come to say—haf you any message for the spy before he is hanged dead?" he said, grinning in his spite.

Margery gasped with fear, and held to 'Beth.

"Not hanged! He is no spy; he only came to see us. We are engaged to one another."

"He came disguised. His companions are making war on us. It is enough. In ten minutes he will be hanged. They are taking him out now. Would you like to see?"

"No, no! Do not kill him. Earn our gratitude. Be generous. Be kind, and let me like you."

And the girl knelt at his feet, and caught at one of the man's rough hands, and kissed it in her agony of fear.

"What will you do suppose I do not kill him? Will you marry me?"

A TALE OF THE BOER WAR.

"She couldn't marry *you*," cried 'Beth, scornfully, and the Boer's teeth showed as he grinned angrily.

"I am as good as any two Englishmen, and better," he said. "In ten minutes he will be hanged. See!"

And he dragged Margery into the open, and pointed to where, a little way off, Gilbert stood under a beam erected for the purpose, with a rope round his neck, half-a-dozen strong Boers standing around, two of whom held the end of the rope, ready to pull their prisoner off the ground

"Gilbert!" she cried.

"Good-bye, and God bless you. Remember I die loving you!" he called back, and she fell almost faint into 'Beth's arms.

"Now, shall I give the word, or will you marry me?" asked Van Leer.

"I'll—oh! I'll marry you," she faltered, bursting into tears.

"Kiss me, then, my leetle wife, so that he can see, or up he goes."

"You cowardly brute! You vile tyrant!" cried 'Beth indignantly.

"Thanks, dear sister-in-law. I shall kiss you one day. Now, Margy, kiss me, or he swings."

Margery staggered towards him, and he caught her in his arms, while Gilbert struggled vainly and frantically to reach them.

Then the girl raised her head to kiss him, but instead fell a dead weight in his arms, fainting.

He carried her back to the little house, and laid her on the bed there.

"It will do. I take the will for the deed. Take care of her, little 'Beth, because she will be very fond of me one day. I must go and tell the spy to congratulate me. He will be so glad he is alive. Ach! what a happy day!"

And he strolled out, leaving 'Beth speechless with anger.

"Never mind, Margy," she said to her sister, as Margery began to recover consciousness. "Our friends will rescue us before that brute is many days older."

Gilbert was thrown back into his prison after having first been told the news that Margery was going to marry the Commandant.

He understood the situation, and could see how pressure had been put on the poor girl; but he would sooner have died than that Margery should ever kiss such a ruffian as Van Leer.

There was still hope that his friends might arrive in time, yet he knew their task was a heavy one.

They had odds to face—more than he cared to reckon. Yet, still, hope was not extinct.

* * * *

The "Nautilus," after leaving her harbour, travelled at slow speed and beneath the surface.

She was timed to reach the privateer about two hours before the Boers usually rose for breakfast, and so there was plenty of time.

The creek was easily found, and onward crept the British submarine, looking out for her rival.

At last the privateer was to be seen, sunk in five fathoms of water for safety, with, of course, part of her crew—or all—on board, so that it was impossible to board or carry her—one advantage the submarine has over an ordinary vessel.

Within a hundred yards of her the "Nautilus" stopped, and soon a dozen men, with Bob, all clad in diving-dresses, emerged in groups of three from the conning-tower hatch, and descended to the bottom of the creek, bearing a coir rope, for Captain Deane was afraid that a steel one might seriously damage the privateer's propeller and ruin her.

It was a weird sight, this procession of men along the sandy floor of the sea, carrying a rope that, moved by the tide, twisted and squirmed like a great sea-serpent.

Soon they reached the privateer, and, aided by a leaden weight, managed to throw the rope over the propeller, and then to give it several turns round, leaving the slack for the propeller to pick up for itself.

Then the procession turned back, headed by Bob.

But hardly had they gone any distance, when the lad stepped backward, pointing, and in evident fear.

Deane, who was in command of the party, moved forward, and peered through the muddy water, stirred by many feet.

A huge spider-crab, standing at least three feet high on its hairy legs, was clashing its mandibles at them, and although it might not have been able to kill one of them with its bite, yet it could tear the diving-suit and bring death to them that way.

Taking an axe from his belt, he rushed at it, hoping to drive it away.

But the creature, not frightened, flew at him.

He struck out, and a lucky blow

sent it down, when others, among whom was Bob, despatched it.

Nothing more hideous exists, and it was with a shudder that Bob passed the corpse, glad to get back.

Half-an-hour later the "Nautilus" was gliding up the creek past the privateer, on her way to find a favourable place for landing her party.

CHAPTER XVIII.

CAPTAIN BALLANCE and his men were not idle after their comrades had left them.

The captain, wounded as he was, decided to reconnoitre the ground in front, and to this end he had a hammock slung between two men, and, accompanied by petty officer Oliver, late gunner to the "St. George," he was carried a couples of miles out.

"This is where they'll place their gun," he said, as they reached the peaky summit of a hill well protected by loose boulders. "It commands our fort, and they can take their time in knocking us to atoms."

"I could hit our fort every time from here, sir,' said Oliver.

"I think you could, Oliver. They won't be so smart, but they'll hit us sometimes; and one hit will about finish us."

"'Tain't much good manning a fort to be used up as targets, sir. I'd sooner be picked off while I had a chance of hitting back."

"I think that's how we all feel, Oliver, and I'm not so sure that we'll man the fort after all."

"There's some nice cover here, sir."

"Yes, but they could outflank us in an hour. Still, we must try something. I shall leave you in charge of the sangars."

"Aye, aye, sir," answered Oliver, but not at all cheerfully.

"I want the men who are to man the sangars to make a display in front of the fort on the approach of the enemy.

"Run in and out of the fort several times when they see you, so that

they'll think there are a lot of you. I shan't leave any other men behind."

"Aye, aye, sir."

"As soon as the Boers are ready to fire, each party manning the sangars will leave the fort and get into the sangars. I hope you will have made the Boers believe that we have left a large number in charge of the fort."

"Aye, aye, sir," said Oliver, showing a little more interest.

"Well, get back and leave me here. I want the men who were to man the fort to double up to me here, and leave the fort empty. Get back as quickly as you can."

"Aye, aye, sir," and Oliver saluted and hurried back.

An hour afterwards the rest of the men joined Captain Ballance, who turned to the right and led the way to a hill a thousand yards away from the one they expected the Boers to utilise.

The range-finder gave the distance as 940 yards, and the captain saw every rifle properly sighted for that distance.

"Now, my lads," said he, "remember that no one fires without orders, even though the Boers are under the muzzles of your rifles. When I tell you to fire, take steady aim, and remember that one shot well directed is worth a dozen badly aimed. Take your time. Now get under cover, and mind, if I see so much as a nose of a man in five minutes, he shall go back to the fort. You've got to prevent the enemy from seeing you. Now find cover, and remember that the enemy is coming from the west, and will probably march to a line with this hill. You must find cover so that men coming from that direction can't see you."

The bluejackets, delighted at the prospect of a fight, more especially those who had so lately been Boer prisoners, found cover easily enough among many boulders lying around, and waited, talking to each other in whispers, while their captain, stoically bearing the pain of his wound, watched for the approach of the foe.

It was quite two hours later when a " hush " went round the watchers.

A dozen Boers, with rifles on their shoulders, were seen coming leisurely over the distant heights, evidently scouts.

Then followed others, and then was heard the heavy rumble of wheels, followed by the crack of a whip.

" Have they oxen? " wondered Captain Ballance, as he saw the foremost Boers draw near, reach the hill he had inspected, group together talking, and then halt.

Soon the gun came in sight, pulled by British prisoners, forty of fifty in number, accompanied by Boers, who were threatening with the whip, if not actually striking them.

A growl of anger passed round among the watchers.

" Britons never shall be slaves," and yet it was maddening to see.

And horny hands grasped their rifles tighter, while fingers itched to pull a trigger.

Straining and halting, checked here and there, yet overcoming the difficulties, toiled the human team, and then came a sudden halt.

Apparently they had refused to pull any more, for a Boer came up, and with a pistol shot two of the unarmed men, and threatened the rest.

But these stood stolid, and even the lash did not move more than one, who sprang at a Boer and knocked him down.

The poor fellow was instantly shot, but it was apparent that the prisoners would do no more.

Indeed, they had just heard that the gun was to be used to attack their countrymen, and one and all had told the Boers that they would die before helping it into position.

Soon they were marched back, and a number of stalwart Boers moved the gun up to the foot of the hill, and after much difficulty, got it into position just behind the brow.

The sailors with Captain Ballance were eagerly watching their commander's face for a sign, but he lay there quietly.

Save that now and again his face twitched with pain, he might have been sleeping, so calm was he.

At the fort the sailors were running to and fro as if in dire consternation, and the Boers could be seen laughing at what they thought was the fright of the British.

Oliver was certainly doing his work well, and, as faces could not be seen so far off, there might have been a couple of hundred men with him, instead of a dozen, for all the Boers could tell.

Boom!

The gun spoke, and a shell went high over the fort.

" Can't shoot for nuts! " whispered a young A.B.

" They'd miss the earth if the shell didn't fall on it," muttered his companion; and then the captain looked round, and there was silence.

The next shot was over, and the next went wide.

The next three hit the ground around the fort, and then came a well-directed shot that hit the fort and burst.

There was a shout of joy from the Boers, but they did not advance yet, but continued firing until the fort was hit seven times.

They apparently thought that they could take it now, for, spreading out and taking cover, they advanced, leaving a guard of about forty men with the gun.

The attacking force had advanced a couple of thousand yards when the defenders of the two sangars began firing.

A party of Boers made a rush for the one on the left, but a dozen of them fell, and the rest sought cover and fired on the defenders.

" 'Tention! " said Captain Ballance quietly. " Independent firing. Pick off the men at the gun, and aim steadily."

The Boers with the gun were unsuspecting.

They were smoking and watching

their comrades, when of a sudden two fell.

They looked to the front, thinking the bullets had come from that direction, when five more dropped, and bullets came whistling around.

They ran for shelter, and the blue-jackets at the same time raced for the gun.

They were quite near before some of the Boers had recovered from their stampede, and began to fire.

Here and there a bluepacket fell.

But the rest were not to be denied.

They rushed the gun, and were among the Boers with a shout of triumph.

Men fell in a hopeless mix; but in two minutes twenty of the Boers had bolted, six were prisoners, and the rest were killed or wounded.

The gun was quickly loaded and fired at the Boers in front, who, seeing the attack on the gun, were now coming back.

The shell burst well among them and they took cover carefully, intending to pick off the gunners as soon as they could creep nearer.

Now was Oliver's chance, and, advancing with all his men, he opened fire on the Boers, who, attacked on both sides, ran towards the mountain, followed by shell after shell until they were out of range.

The British had lost seven killed and six wounded, but the victory was complete, and the sailors at once began to tow the gun to their fort, now safe by its possession.

At this time the " Nautilus " had passed up the creek, and was landing her men, with a couple of quick-firing guns, about a mile above the Boer camp.

A few of the enemy could be seen on guard, lazily lounging about, while several fires told that cooking was going on.

The tricky Boers were again out-tricked, and were never suspecting the proximity of a British force.

CHAPTER XIX.

COMMANDED by Lieutenant Watkins and Sir Peter, the British crept toward the Boer camp.

A sentry was captured before he could give the alarm, and then, at the double, a party of blue-jackets reached the huts where a large number of British prisoners were kept, mostly merchant sailors, and a few passengers.

Then a screech from the Boer women gave the alarm, and in another two minutes a waggon with the Geneva Cross was seen to be hurried out of the camp, drawn by a number of Boer women, while the men, after firing a few shots, bolted in another direction.

" Now to release the girls and Mr. Romer," said Sir Peter, as his men sent a few volleys at long range after the retreating Boers, " and don't fire on the ambulance, men, whatever you do."

An elderly man stepped forward.

" There go my daughters. I beg you will lose no time. These people are very vicious, and may harm them out of spite. I will show the way," and he tried to run forward.

" Professor Grant, may I ask ? " inquired Sir Peter, kindly, offering his arm to the worn old man.

" Yes, sir; but for Heaven's sake send your men on. They are in that hut," he answered, pointing out the hut that had the little garden.

Lieutenant Watkins and a few men doubled to it, and went in, coming out afterwards with the cry: " The place is empty."

" Hunt everywhere, call for them, shout, men !" cried the professor, frantically.

Bob, who had gone ahead of the others to look for his uncle, came running back.

" Uncle has been taken away as well as the girls," he called out.

" In the ambulance," said Sir Peter, excitedly. " Dolt that I was not to suppose that they would use the Geneva Cross to cover their mischief. Come, men, double up after them."

Several of the men started, the waggon being now a little more than a mile away, when a big Boer, followed by several others, was seen to overtake it. He pointed his rifle at the waggon, and made signs that if the pursuit was continued, he would fire on the occupants.

"He'll do it. It's Van Leer. Don't pursue them; it's our only chance!" cried the professor, wringing his hands. "Oh! my girls, my girls, so near liberty."

"We'll stalk them, professor, and rush their laager in the night," said Sir Peter, cheerily.

"And Uncle Gil's with them, I feel sure, and he'll protect them," said Bob.

"Is he a prisoner too? Oh! they are too cunning for us. They are never to be depended upon. That man Van Leer is utterly unprincipled. Please do not lose sight of the waggon," and the professor staggered forward and fell, so weak was he.

They carried him to the "Nautilus," where Captain Deane made him comfortable.

Bob, who returned with him, promised him never to leave the pursuit until the girls were recovered, when, looking up at the screen, he saw a small dark object depicted, moving on it.

"Look, Captain Deane. Is that the privateer?" he asked, quickly.

Deane looked; the shadow was moving towards them, and growing bigger.

Now it looked like a small fish—a minnow—but the minnow was growing.

"Screw up the hatch—quickly!" shouted the skipper, rushing to his keyboard.

A couple of hands were in the conning-tower in a moment, the hatch screwed down, and obedient to the command of the telegraph the "Nautilus" sank, and then turned so as to meet the privateer bows on.

"They must have found the cable, and got it loose, before their propeller was jammed. Now, I fear, it means fighting or being destroyed," said Deane, gravely.

"Then, of course, we'll fight," said Bob, "only I know that if Sir Peter were here he'd wish us to avoid a battle. Can't we hide?"

The picture on the screen was growing; the minnow had become a salmon in size.

"They are bound to cruise with the conning-tower above water," said Deane, after a pause. "They can't see under as we do. There's a deep hole a little way from here; I'll try to hide in that."

The "Nautilus" sped forward at full speed, and the picture on the screen grew with such rapidity that Bob found himself holding on to the table, fearing the shock of what seemed to be the inevitable collision.

Tap! tap! went the keys, and the "Nautilus" stopped, and then sank like a stone. All lights were at the same instant turned out, so that nothing should guide the enemy.

The water even here was shallow, and a moment later there was a grating sound, and a slight quivering of the "Nautilus."

The bottom of the privateer had just touched her as she passed over, and concealment was useless.

If she could turn the privateer could use her torpedo, and Captain Deane determined that she should not turn, if he could help it.

The "Nautilus" could turn in her own length, and she was quickly round and alongside the privateer, just as that vessel had got half way round.

Swinging his vessel bow and stern alongside the privateer, Deane allowed that vessel to manœuvre as she pleased.

Round and round in narrow circles they sped, the iron sides grating against each other.

Then, with a bound, the privateer would attempt to get ahead, only to find the speedier vessel in her old place a second after.

Then the Boers would go astern, but ahead or astern, or circling any way, they could not shake off the "Nautilus," and Bob laughed at their attempts, and pictured the Boers swearing at their ill-success.

They were now over the hole wherein the "Nautilus" had tried to hide, and here the privateer stopped, as though the Boers were sulky.

"I wish Sir Peter were here," said

Captain Deane; "he knows the tricks of these Boers. I wonder what they're up to next?"

"I expect that's just what they're wondering," said Bob, laughing, as he caressed Waif, who had now grown into a silky-coated dog, in splendid condition.

"I don't like their inaction; they've some plan on hand. Stand by!" he telegraphed to the engine-room.

The lights were now full on, and the X rays showed every plate and every rivet in the side of the privateer.

Both vessels had their conning-towers high out of water, and below them was, perhaps, sixty feet of water, before the mud was reached.

Suddenly the stern of the privateer sank rapidly, and almost before Captain Deane could telegraph his orders, her nose was pointing upward, close to the "Nautilus."

"Full speed astern!" telegraphed Deane, for it was almost impossible to sink rapidly enough to avoid the torpedo that he knew was about to be delivered, and as the "Nautilus" backed, the fish-like weapon darted from the bows of the enemy, just missing the British vessel.

It leapt into the air, and fell back with a splash, and then darted into the bank, where it exploded, shaking the submarines, and sending a great wave over the banks of the creek.

"A narrow escape," said Bob, cooly, as he quickly comprehended the attack and its failure.

Captain Deane did not reply. Obedient to his commands, the "Nautilus" half turned, and then sank.

There was a grating of iron as she touched the privateer, and a quiver as the privateer's screw lashed the water in her efforts to escape from her position.

"Tell Buchan to fill all water tanks, please, Bob," Captain Deane said, and Bob ran into the engine-room, and a moment after heard the water rushing in.

"We're on top of her, aren't we?" Buchan asked.

"Yes, and the captain's getting in as much weight as possible, so as to drive her nicely into the mud," Bob replied.

"She can't use her torpedo tubes then?"

"No, and she can't get fresh air."

"No more can we."

"Oh! yes we can," cried Bob. "We can get tubes out to the top."

"Divers required," called out Captain Deane, and Bob hurried back to him.

CHAPTER XX.

THE big gun taken from the Boers was soon peeping over the stone walls of the fort, and Captain Ballance, his wound dressed, was resting uneasily as the time of twilight approached.

The lack of night had been distressing for all the wounded, some of whom could not sleep well in the constant light, and just now the want of darkness was more noticeable, for the volcano was flaring continuously, and sending flames and fiery smoke, that lit up the heavens.

The wind was howling outside, laden with fine snow, which seemed to penetrate through every wrap the sentries wore, so that Petty Officer Oliver, ever alert, made his rounds more frequent, lest any should fall asleep.

Dense clouds were scurrying overhead, and a semblance of night, although made lurid by the flames of the mountain, began to soothe the fevered eyes of the wounded men, and Captain Ballance dozed, and dreamed that ever-recurring nightmare of the submarine destroying his noble vessel.

He felt the shock of the explosion over again; he saw the men hurrying to their quarters to meet the unforeseen foe, as steady as British sailors ever are.

He saw the vessel sinking beneath his feet, and felt himself once again swimming in the dark waters that were overwhelming his brave comrades, and then he awoke shivering.

"It's very dark," he thought, for the volcano was now only spouting out huge clouds of black smoke that added to the general darkness. "How it blows. I'll try and stand," and stiffly and sorely he reached the ground.

Then he thought that he would see how the watch was kept, and throwing his coat over his shoulders, and pulling his cap over his eyes, he stepped beyond the shelter the men had rigged up for him within the walls.

A gust of wind nearly drove him back, and the frozen particles of snow whipped his face and forced back his breath.

"Who goes there?" called out a sentry, stepping from behind a buttress, as the captain turned into the open ground.

"St. George," hailed the captain, giving the password, and then: "It's a cold night to-night. Keep moving, my man, or you'll be frozen."

"Aye, aye, sir," said the man, a little shamefacedly, for he had been sheltering behind the angle of the walls, and Captain Ballance moved on.

The darkness was so deep now that after a pace or two he lost sight of the sentry.

Now and again there was a lull, and during one of these he thought that he heard a voice speaking gutterally, unlike the British tongue.

It struck him that this was just such a night as an enemy might choose for an attack, and he peered into the darkness, hoping to see, yet unable to penetrate the gloom.

A stone rolled down at some little distance off.

He was sure now that someone was about near the fort, and he hurried back.

The sentry was walking briskly up and down, and he sent him to call in the other sentries, and Oliver, who was going his rounds.

Then he returned to the fort, and woke all excepting the wounded men, and silently all took up their positions, rifles in hand.

Oliver, with the four sentries, came in with the news that the barbed wire had already been cut, so that the Boers meant to attack soon, and had, unseen, cleared the obstacles that would hinder a sudden rush.

Two of the wounded men insisted on rising, and these had instructions to light the lamps as soon as the first shot was fired.

It was nervous work waiting, when no one could see ten yards away, and none could tell on which side or sides the attack would be made.

Men wanted to know that their comrades were still standing near them; some had a violent inclination to cough; some could not keep their feet still, but not one man among the gallant sailors wished to be out of the coming fight.

Suddenly a bright glare lit up the fort, and dazzled the eyes of the defenders without illuminating the darkness outside. The walls were rather more than breast high, and the electric searchlight brought up by the Boers showed every defender without disclosing themselves.

"Duck, men!" shouted Captain Ballance, and instinctively most of the men stooped under the shelter of the wall, as a rattling volley struck down two out of those who had not been quick enough.

The bullets were coming from three sides of the fort, and the Boers could be heard shouting to each other encouragement, together with terrible threats against the British.

The lamps had scarcely been lighted when they were shot down, and Captain Ballance told Oliver to lead the men out at the back, the only side not attacked, and to take what shelter he could outside, for the fort was untenable.

"Then fire at the electric light and those underneath it," he added.

Hardly had Oliver and his men got out than the Boers made the final rush.

They had hesitated somewhat on finding such slight opposition, fearing a trap, but seeing the gun they valued so highly still in its place, they rushed for it after a little hesitation.

In the fort were Captain Ballance, two of the sailors who had refused to leave him, and the wounded, two of whom had taken up rifles.

These five fired on the first of the Boers as they came climbing over the parapet, or standing up to it and firing in, and several of the Boers fell dead or wounded, but in a moment the gallant band were shot or struck down, and the Boers were in possession of the fort.

Some of their men threatened to shoot the wounded, but a few of the older Boers forbade it, one even standing across the body of Captain Ballance, as he lay bleeding from a wound in his head.

The gun was at once hauled out into the open the searchlight lending its assistance, for the path was rocky and difficult.

This was just what Oliver had been waiting for, and when the gun had been dragged about fifty yards, and almost every Boer present was engaged in pulling or pushing it over an abrupt incline, he gave the order to fire, and his men, who had been anxiously hoping for their opportunity, sent in a telling volley, which scattered the enemy, quite a number of them falling.

The light was now turned on to the height, where Oliver and his men were, leaving the Boers in darkness, and a pattering of bullets round the sailors made them stick to cover.

"Fire at the light!" was Oliver's order now, for he knew that the Boers would outflank him in a short time, and, aided by the light, they would be able to pick out his men, while they had no chance of retaliating.

Shot after shot was fired at the lantern, but perhaps, owing to the boisterous wind, perhaps in consequence of the dazzling rays, not a shot got home.

"We must charge down, lads, and smash it up," cried Oliver. "Short rushes in the centre, and the last ten on the left of the line work round to the left and get into the shadow, and make a good rush from there. The light can't cover a long line all the time."

The order was promptly obeyed, but not without loss, although the bad weather spoilt the enemy's shooting, for fingers were so numbed now that they could hardly feel the rifle.

On the left, led by a young A.B., who took charge naturally, a few men worked out of the light for a moment or two, and then, before the lantern could be turned upon them, they rushed the half-dozen Boers working the light, threw down the pole on which the lantern was fixed, and smashed the lantern and the engine.

It was now so dark that firing ceased, by mutual consent, for it was impossible to tell friend from foe.

The successful party groped their way back, seeking for wounded on the way, and bringing in two of their own men and one Boer, while Oliver carried in the rest.

On mustering the party in the fort, nine were found to be missing, and seven wounded were brought in, also another later on, when a search party was sent out.

Captain Ballance, though severely hurt, was not dead, but the accommodation for so many wounded men was very inadequate, and there being no surgeon there, a young sailor, who had some knowledge of binding wounds, had to do the best he could for the gallant fellows, some of whom, bad as they were, tried to make light of their wounds.

The storm lasted for nearly six hours, everyone of which was long with anxiety, and then came the grey light again, and Oliver, with a few of the men, went out to see what had become of the gun.

They saw it not a couple of hundred yards away, and, approaching from the other side, were a number of Boers, who had also evidently come to take possession of it, and to demolish the fort altogether.

CHAPTER XXI.

HAVING left the "Nautilus" in charge of ten men, with Buchan in command, Sir Peter, with Captain Deane (who, with Bob and the rest of the crew, had landed in the diving-suits) and the released prisoners, pushed on and freed another seventy prisoners, the remainder of them having been taken away to the mountains by the Boers after they had dragged the big gun, where also Gilbert Romer and the two girls had been removed.

The men who were released were armed, with the exception of eight who were on the sick list, and who were left behind, and to the number of nearly 130 the little army began to march across country towards the fort built over the creek.

Bob was promised that as soon as those in the fort had been relieved and added to the very small British army, the country should be searched until his uncle and the girls were found, and before leaving the camp Sir Peter wrote out a notice addressed to the Boers, to the effect that if any British subject in their hands was killed, any person or persons ordering his death, or killing him, or being present at his death, would be executed by the British forces now in the island.

An old Boer who was found hiding near the camp was given a copy of this, and told to hand it to the Commandant, and to read it to every Boer he came across.

The old rascal swore that he was not a Boer, but had been captured by them and forced to accompany Van Leer; but he shambled off with the notice, and, finding that he was not followed, made straight for the mountain.

The march across country was for a long time uneventful; but as the party drew nearer to their destination the sounds of distant firing were heard, for some of the enemy were using black powder.

A couple of wounded Boers, evidently making for their camp, fell into the hands of the British.

These were interrogated by Sir Peter, and from them he heard that most of the British had been killed, their fort demolished, and that the Boers, with their big gun, could destroy any force without coming within rifle-shot; and as the British had no big gun, of course resistance was useless.

"How came you two to be wounded," asked Sir Peter, bluntly, "if you can kill all the British without being under fire yourselves?"

"Dreachery," grunted one of the prisoners. "Dey drick us dey surrender, and den fire on us."

"You're telling a lie," said Sir Peter, coolly. "The British fight fairly, as you know. Where is your big gun? I suppose you've lost it?" he added, hazarding a guess.

"We haf god id bag," said the surly Boer.

"So you lost it once to men whom you said couldn't fire on you. And you'll lose it again, my friends. Your day is up. We'll have no more privateering, no more shooting of sentries or small bodies of men. You shall have the same liberty as any British subject when you can behave as one, and if you do behave well, you'll find that no nation in the world is so free as the British."

A grunt answered this oration, and the party proceeded until the firing became louder, though not so continuous.

They found the ridge where the big fight for the gun had been, with plenty of evidence of the battle, and from this point they could see the firing in the distance; but the big gun was silent.

They could just see it, and apparently it lay between the opposing forces.

And once they saw a party of Boers rush forward to seize it, and then fall back with loss.

"We want to cut off the retreat of those fellows, who will run off to the mountain on seeing us," exclaimed Sir Peter. "If, Lieutenant Watkins, you will lead a party round to the left, and give the signal to advance when you are in position, we shall net the lot."

"I think it the best plan, Sir

Peter. Volunteers!" cried the lieutenant. And a number of men having offered, he chose forty of them, and, under cover of the woods, marched off, while the others watched the battle beyond.

* * * *

The contending sides were both well entrenched now, and neither made much impression on the other, although the Boers outnumbered the British by at least ten to one.

But they had found that Captain Ballance's men shot very straight, and they did not intend to take any risks, hoping that the British would shoot away their ammunition and become an easy prey.

And First Class Petty Officer Oliver was at that very time worrying because he saw that this must soon come about.

He and his men were treasuring their cartridges now, only shooting when the Boers tried to rush closer or gain a new shelter a little nearer to the fort.

"Don't surrender, Oliver," Captain Ballance told him. "When you've fired your last cartridge, fix bayonets, and when they rush the fort charge into them. Remember that the fewer we leave for our friends the better their chance."

"We can give a good account of ourselves yet, sir," replied Oliver. "I think they'll be pretty sick of fighting by the time we're done for."

"Thank all the men for me, Oliver," said the captain, trying to raise himself, and sinking back exhausted by the effort. "I wish I could stand with you. Tell them I am proud of them. Tell them that some day those at home will learn of their last stand and be proud of them. There's not one thinking of surrender, I hope, Oliver?"

"Not one, sir," cried Oliver, heartily. "If there was, I'd bayonet him, even if he was my own brother."

"I don't believe in throwing lives away, Oliver; I can't bear to see my brave fellows fall." And tears filled the gallant officer's eyes. "But now it is our duty to die."

"We'll die, sir, so as you won't be ashamed of us, and God bless you,

sir. The men are only sorry you can't lead our last charge."

"I think I could, Oliver, if you gave me an arm."

"Not you, sir. You'd be a dead weight on me, and prevent me from having my bit. Men!" Oliver called out. "Before it's too late, three cheers for our captain."

Three rousing cheers startled the Boers, and all who heard wondered what success had been gained that should result in such cheering. The Boers who were preparing for the rush on the fort held off, suspicious that the British had somehow obtained reinforcements, and for half an hour they lay quiet.

At last Sir Peter saw the agreed signal from Lieutenant Watkins, and ordered the advance, Bob, at his urgent request, being allowed to go forward at the double with Bill Yeo and five ship's boys who had been among the prisoners.

"The young beggars can push a long way ahead of us," Sir Peter said to Captain Deane, who was beside him. "Young limbs don't tire easily, and their lungs are in better working order than the winds of we old 'uns."

"They're all plucky lads, and it may be they'll make a useful diversion," answered Deane, as the boys spread out and sprinted forward as though they had only a hundred yards to cover.

"Yes, and Bob is sensible; he'll see that they take cover. Gad, I hope he will push on. Those fellows yonder are gathering for a rush, I can see, and they'll have the fort before we can reach them; and we may have difficulty in turning them out. Some of you men double in support of the boys."

Several of the younger men did so, but close confinement and half-rations had weakened those who had been prisoners, and most of them had to be content with a steady advance, for the most athletic of the sailors were with the lieutenant.

The Boers were firing rapidly now, the British in the fort hardly replying, and the enemy were closing up quickly in short rushes.

"Shout, men," called out Sir Peter, hoping that he could attract the

Boers' attention and stop the attack; but the voices were too far away, or the Boers were too busy with those in front to look behind them.

"Bob's started. He's meaning to let them see him," said Captain Deane, as he watched the lad take careful aim from the top of a rock and fire. The distance was still too great, however, and the Boers did not notice the attack.

Bob spurted on again, he and Bill Yeo racing side by side, while the others came on after them at intervals.

A party of Boers had gathered behind a ridge some twenty yards below the level of the fort, and about fifty yards away, when Oliver and his men pushed a great boulder from the top of the wall upon which they had managed to hoist it, so that it went bounding among the attacking forces, accompanied by a number of stones and small rocks that it had detached as it leapt down.

It was only a momentary check for the enemy, but it enabled Bob and his companion to gain another couple of hundred yards; and then, as they saw the Boers again nerving themselves for the rush, the two lads fired.

This time the bullets, or one of them, hit the rocks near the Boers, and several turned round.

Bob fired again, and, some of the other boys coming up, also discharged their weapons quickly, the distance being too great for accurate shooting.

They could see the consternation in the Boer ranks, for a number of the enemy came hurrying back and took up new positions, in order to protect their rear.

The main body under Sir Peter at this time had just reached the top of a ridge, and the cheer they gave was heard by the Boers, who saw that the fort was sure to be relieved, and who immediately began to withdraw inland as fast as possible, as Sir Peter had expected.

They had not gone a mile, however, before they were seen to halt and seek cover.

Lieutenant Watkins's column was now engaging them, and, as Sir Peter was rapidly advancing, the position of the Boers was perilous, for foes were upon three sides of them and the sea on the fourth.

They retreated again, and while some took cover to oppose the advancing British, the rest prepared to rush the fort, and thus put themselves in a stronger position.

"They will take it, too, for our poor fellows are evidently out of ammunition," said Sir Peter, as he lay down and took a careful shot at a Boer who was firing at him a thousand yards away.

"Look at that, Sir Peter," Deane said, pointing towards the cliffs.

Bob and his lads had reached the edge of the cliffs, and were going over.

"They're going to try and get round to the fort by the cliffs in time," said Sir Peter. "Good boys! May they do it, and, anyhow, they deserve success. It's a smart move, and if Bob lives he'll be a rich man."

And the millionaire, taking aim, again fired, and noted that the bullet struck the rock ten yards below the Boer.

"I'm getting a poor shot," he said; "but I've often made a bull after one trial shot." And he loaded again.

CHAPTER XXII.

WHEN Gilbert Romer was taken up country he had no knowledge that his fiancée and her sister were travelling in one of the waggons just ahead.

His escort hurried him on, and after a time made him assist in hauling a waggon, for there being no horses on the island, all haulage had to be done by men.

The work was hard, but after a time the party were joined by the prisoners who had drawn the big gun, and then the Boers gave up work and marched beside these men, whom they treated as slaves, using the whip freely.

On anyone showing a sign of rebellion, a rifle was promptly pointed at him, with an oath or a threat; and the British, knowing that their countrymen were now endeavouring to procure their release, chose to continue the degrading toil sooner than die when the tables might so shortly be turned on their captors.

Van Leer took his place beside the waggon which held Margery and 'Beth, to the intense disgust of both.

He had been drinking heavily, and was more than usually brutal in tone and manner.

"You are too pretty to be an Englishman's wife," he said to Margery, with a leer. "You will make me a beautiful wife."

She made no answer, and the contemptuous silence angered him.

"Ach! You are so anxious to kiss me again, I see. How you did kiss—so strongly, as if to say, 'Van Leer, how I love you.'"

"I hate and despise you," Margery said, stung to speech.

"You say so, my pretty, but you do not mean it. Come and kiss me again. You shall. Halt, there!" And the column halted. "This lady wants the prisoners to see how much she prefers an Africander to a miserable rooinek."

He pulled her out of the waggon roughly, but without violence, and, despite her struggles, half carried, half led her to one side where all could see.

Gilbert saw Margery shrinking, and her eyes seemed to implore his assistance.

He let go of the rope he was holding, and edged round.

His guards were all looking at their leader, some indifferent, some laughing, a few—a very few—ashamed of their countryman.

"Now, once again, kiss me," Van Leer cried, "or I'll hang him," he whispered.

And the girl put up her hands before her eyes, loathing the sight of him.

"I'll kiss you first. That is what you are waiting for," he said; and taking her in his powerful arms, he kissed her.

Gilbert, mad with rage, slipped past his guards, and ran empty-handed at the tyrant.

Two or three of the Boers fired at him, but in the hurry missed him, and he threw himself upon Van Leer, tore Margery, who had fainted away, from the ruffian, only to fall a moment later, as Van Leer knocked him senseless with a crashing blow from the butt-end of his rifle.

"Shoot the dog!" he called out. And then, as several rifles were raised, "No, no, it is too good for him. Tie him up and put him in a waggon. Tell me when he can speak."

Gilbert was thrown into a waggon like a sack, and a rope hitched round his ankles, and Margery being once more carefully placed in the vehicle she had left, the party went on.

It was heavy going now, over rocky ground, and always uphill, as they ascended the first part of the mountain.

In four hours they had reached the caves, where Van Leer reckoned that he could best make a stand, and into these the prisoners were hurried.

Gilbert was still insensible, and two of the Boers, more kindly dispositioned than the others, carried him into a cave adjoining that set aside for the girls, while Van Leer was busily engaged elsewhere.

Margery and 'Beth were bathing his head when Gilbert came to, wondering where he was and what had happened; Margery, on her knees be-

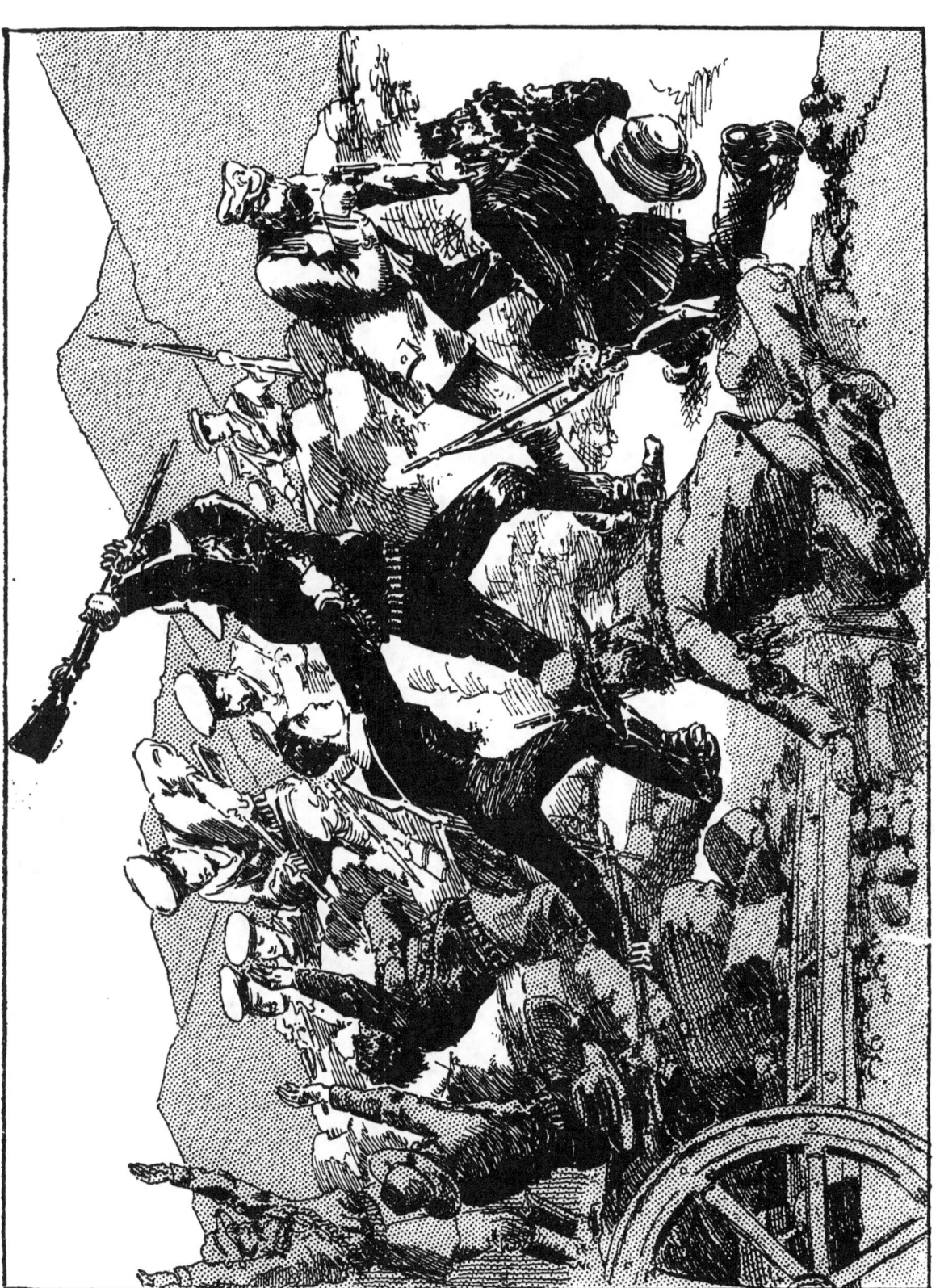

"BOB THREW HIS ARMS ROUND ONE DESPERATE FELLOW."

No. 5.

side him, kissed his forehead, and he felt her tears fall upon his face.

"Margery," he said faintly, and she kissed him again. "Margery, are you safe?"

"Quite safe," she said, "and you are dreadfully hurt."

"No, dearest; only a little. See, I can get up."

And he rose and walked, a little dizzily at first, but more strongly after a minute or two.

"I wish I had a pistol. I'd shoot Van Leer," 'Beth said angrily, and he smiled a little.

"It would do no good, 'Beth. You two are safe, for our friends are sure to be here soon," he said, making a pretence of hopefulness he was far from feeling.

"Yes, but they said they'd shoot you. Oh, darling, now is our time. No one is watching. Cannot you hide from them? These caves seem endless," Margery cried, clinging to him.

"Yes; do try," 'Beth urged. "I will look after Margery. Some of the Boers are not unkind to us, and won't let Van Leer harm us; but they have no sympathy for you."

"Perhaps you are right. I could not bear to die and leave you, dear one." And Gilbert embraced the girl once again.

"Quick, then. Let me see first."

And Margery stepped out of the cave.

It was very dark there, but where the light streamed in the Boers were busy taking in provisions and making ready for a siege. The other way was empty.

"Go as far as you can. Hide until we come," Margery urged.

"And here are some biscuits they gave us and we couldn't eat," kind-hearted 'Beth said, forcing into his hands what was to have been their supper. "Now go, if you love Margery."

"God bless you both. Farewell for a little while, Margery."

And once more Gilbert embraced her, and then crept into the darkness, feeling the wall as he did so.

He had gone a hundred yards or so when he heard a stone he had kicked fall a long distance.

He very cautiously felt forward, and found a big gap.

He dropped a stone, and he heard it strike the bottom quite a long way down.

He tried to creep around, but apparently the abyss was right across the cave; and it was doubtless the knowledge that escape was barred by it that had caused the Boers to guard the girls' cave so little.

He felt like a rat in a trap. As soon as the Boers missed him they would search this cave, and find him sitting on the brink of this pit.

Would it not be better to escape from their anger and fling himself down? He was so tired. He ached in every bone.

But Margery? No, that would be cowardice. He would at least stand by her as long as he could.

Still, as he could not escape, he might as well pass as much time as possible with her; and so he turned, and still feeling the wall—but the wall on the other side of the cave this time—he began to retire.

A little way up he felt a ledge, which seemed to go along some way, at least a foot wide.

He felt it back again to the edge of the abyss, and it did not stop there, but turned round.

He decided to try if it would lead him to some hiding-place, and so he climbed up to it and cautiously advanced.

The intense darkness perhaps saved him from slipping, for not only did he advance very carefully, but he did not see that he was on a great wall, with a drop of three hundred feet below him.

At times the ledge was only four inches wide, but he clung to the wall and slowly passed on, the path continually rising.

For over an hour he kept along it, and then it broadened, and he found himself on a floor of sand.

Still following the wall, he came to an opening with a sandy floor, and away in the distance was a speck of light.

In another ten minutes he was out in the open air on the side of the mountain looking towards the east, the Boers having entered on the south side.

CHAPTER XXIII.

WHEN Bob, with Bill Yeo, and the ship's boys found that a strong force of Boers had faced round to prevent their advance, while the main body of the enemy prepared to rush the fort, they were for a little while non-plussed.

It was Bill who first suggested working round by the cliffs.

"You see, Master Bob," he said, "we can keep under the edge, so we won't be seen. There's a path goes along. It's a bit up and downy, but it's pretty safe."

"But, supposing the Boers get into the fort first," suggested Bob.

"They won't be expecting us, and when our folk attack in front, wouldn't it be a lovely diversion, Master Bob, to pop up serenely from behind, and astonish them?"

"I think you're right, Bill," said Bob, with the air of a veteran, delighted with the adventure himself.

And that is how it came about, as mentioned in the chapter before last, that the lads disappeared down the cliffs.

Meantime, Chief Petty Officer Oliver had been gathering together all the cartridges he could find, some having been spilt by the fighters, some dropped by wounded men, while ten packets of ten each were found quite unexpectedly under the straw of the bed of a wounded man, who had for some time been grumbling about the stones that were hurting him.

"No surrender, Oliver," said Captain Ballance, as he feebly smiled when the gallant sailor told him with great glee that he and his men had a few more rounds still to fire.

"And a lot of the enemy are moving to the rear, sir. It looks as though our friends are coming that way."

"Or are the enemy beginning to retreat?"

"No, sir; the rest are getting together for the last rush. I've told the men not to fire until they're but a hundred yards off, and then to use the magazines for as much as is in them. We may stop them, sir."

"Not if they are determined, Oli-ver; but it will make our friends' task easier."

"They're calling me, sir. Good-bye," and Oliver ran to the front, where his men were anxiously waiting the charge.

It seemed as though some of the Boers had great difficulty in screwing up their courage, for nearly an hour had passed since the rush had been threatened, and still they held off.

A few moving specks on the distant hills in front were now plainly visible to the keen-eyed sailors.

"Our chaps are coming, Mr. Oliver," cried one.

"Yes; and we have the beggars between two fires," answered the petty officer cheerily.

"Only our fire's near going out. It's just the cinders," grumbled one sturdy Cockney.

"Cinders make a hot fire at times, Ogg," cried Oliver, and then, after a moment's pause: "Look out, lads, they're coming! Aim low, and aim steady. Don't fire at a man's face, or may be you'll shoot over his head. Independent firing with magazines. Fire!"

The Boers evidently meant business this time, for they came with a rush there was no standing against.

There were considerably over a hundred of them, and though more than twenty fell, the rest reached the fort, and then numbers told.

The gallant sailors, some knocked down, some shot, made a splendid resistance; but for the second time the enemy were in possession of the fort.

Binding the hands of their un-wounded prisoners, and, hastily placing the wounded, Oliver among these, on one side, the Boers began without delay to strengthen the fortifications, and to get in the big gun, and put it in position.

*   *   *   *

The enemy in front of Sir Peter and his party now began to fall back, as on the north side Lieutenant Watkins and his sailors advanced in an endeavour to thrust themselves between the retreating Boers and the fort.

But the Boers, always good in defence, turned their right wing to meet the new attack, and strengthened by a small reinforcement from the fort, they doggedly fell back, fighting every inch of the way, until, as they neared the fort, the rifles of their comrades began to tell in their favour, and the British, having driven them back and prevented a retreat into the interior, now joined forces, while the leaders held a council of war.

Lieutenant Watkins was for an immediate assault on the fort before the enemy had time to strengthen their position.

"Wait until to-night, Mr. Watkins," urged Sir Peter. "I have fought for and against the Boers, and they are bad sentries. They must have sleep, and then will come our time. My advice is, wait for the night."

"But there is no night here," said the lieutenant, somewhat testily. "It's never dark at this time of the year."

"I called it night, because soon must come the time for sleep. Our own men must be weary."

"Not so tired but that they can re-take that fort."

"We might be successful, Mr. Watkins; but at what a cost! We can't afford to lose half of our men in a frontal attack, when we have a good chance of gaining our ends without much loss of life."

"British sailors, Sir Peter, don't count the risk. Nelson went for victory, and didn't mind dying for it," said the young lieutenant, hotly.

"Nor would any man here, I think, Mr. Watkins," Sir Peter said, flushing a little, but keeping cool; "but we have much at stake. We have to meet another commando of Boers—those who have fled to the mountains; these will be sure to entrench, and we shall want every man then."

"I have given my opinion. Our present object is to take that fort, and to capture all the Boers left alive in it," and Mr. Watkins set his lips firmly.

"I haven't said anything yet," remarked Captain Deane, quietly, "because I am not a fighting man, nor have I had any experience with Boers until just lately; but my idea is that Bob's scheme of getting round under the cliffs was a very happy one, and if we wait until the Boers go to sleep, we can send a party—one or two at a time, in order to avoid suspicion—after Bob, with instructions to be ready at, say, four in the morning, and when we start firing, to rush the fort from behind."

"It's a good plan, Deane, if Bob doesn't give it away by showing himself beforehand," said Sir Peter.

"He won't, Sir Peter. That lad isn't a fool, and he's changed a lot lately. Trust him to feel his way. They say scouting is born in some, and it's my belief it's natural to Bob."

"Very well, gentlemen, as you are both against me, I must give in," said Mr. Watkins, "only let us agree that if your *daylight* night surprise fails, that we take the fort by assault."

"Agreed," said Captain Deane.

"Agreed," said Sir Peter, adding: "Will you send twenty of the freshest men to find their way round by the cliffs, and to meet Bob, and let the rest go?"

"And if you permit, I'll go in charge," said Deane.

The lieutenant's lips curled.

"I think, captain," he said, "that Navy men will prefer to be led by a Navy man."

"I think, Mr. Watkins, that if they hint at such a thing, you will be able to tell them that they may be proud to follow the man to whom their deliverance from prison is chiefly due. To whose wonderful pluck and preseverance we all of us owe our lives. No, no, Deane, I insist. You shall go," and Sir Peter held out his hand to Deane.

"I—er—beg Captain Deane's pardon. I am quite prepared to go with him myself, and to serve under him, although the King's regulations——" stammered the lieutenant, evidently ashamed of his attitude.

"You are wanted here, Mr. Watkins. Some of your men have already served under us civilians, and the King's regulations don't run at the South Pole. Kindly tell off twenty men, and good-bye, Deane.

I hope we shall meet in the fort as victors."

The two men said good-bye, and, taking advantage as far as possible of the lay of the land, Captain Deane went to the cliffs, and soon disappeared, the men who were to go with him following at intervals.

Bob and his party had got quite close to the fort when they heard the firing, and then the shouts of the victorious Boers, which only too plainly told the tale of the defeat of the few brave men who had held out for so long and so bravely.

"We'd better go back, Master Bob," whispered Bill Yeo. "We ain't got no earthly chance against a fort full of them chaps."

"You can, if you like, Bill," said Bob. "I'm going to reconnoitre when all is quiet. It seems to me that we could make the attack well from this side."

"I'm with you, Master Bob. I don't go back without you."

"Then I shall wait until all is quiet. If I'm caught, go back and tell Sir Peter that I advise him to send some men at least, to attack from this side."

"Can't I come with you?" pleaded Bill.

"No, Bill. I leave you in command," said Bob, grandiloquently, looking upon his army of six boys.

"Me, captain? Then won't I just lead 'em to death or glory," said Bill, grinning.

"No, you won't, you young idiot," answered Bob. "You'll just lead them safely back, and see Sir Peter."

"I'll do it, Master Bob; trust me."

"I do," said Bob, briefly.

CHAPTER XXIV.

It was midnight before Bob cautiously climbed to the summit of the cliffs near the fort.

The other boys were asleep in a little cave they had found near by, but Bob felt particularly wide awake.

The responsibility of leadership had sobered his boyish spirits greatly, and he was anxious to take no risk that was not absolutely necessary, so that he might be of service later on.

He could see no sentry about, but as he crawled nearer he found one asleep with his back against a stone, and his rifle across his knees.

It was a great temptation to take the rifle and then to capture the man, but the lad restrained himself, and crept closer to the fort.

There were few signs of life there. Occasionally a wounded man groaned, but otherwise all was quiet.

The fort had been strengthened in front; the walls had been made up where knocked down, and built higher in parts, and the big gun peeped from an embrasure.

He crept round, and passed another sleeping sentry, and noticed that a tangle of wire had been stretched across and across the front and the sides of the fort, but although some had been placed in coils at the back, it was not yet laid, the Boers evidently having no fear of an attack from that side.

He was almost tempted to go back and fetch the boys and hold up the sleepers, but he knew that there were desperate men there, and a large number of them who would probably not surrender.

The risk was too great, and he must go back and seek reinforcements.

He made a note of the entanglements, and quietly calculated the number of men who could enter the fort at one time from the rear, and then crept back to where his companions were sleeping.

He woke Bill Yeo, and told him what he was about to do.

"Hadn't I better go, Master Bob," asked Bill, "while you stop here, because p'r'aps the boys wouldn't obey me as they would you?"

"Very well, Bill; you go, and as quickly as you can. Tell Sir Peter to send forty men here, and to make a sham attack in front, and we'll carry the fort."

"Couldn't we surprise it?"

"Yes, if we had the men here now, but not by the time you can fetch them. Hurry off, now," and Bill, leaving his rifle behind, sped along the path where it was broad enough, climbing here, and dropping there, for the way was by no means easy.

He had not gone very far when he saw men a long way below him, whom he took to be Boers.

He was at first inclined to go back, and warn Bob, but on second thoughts he decided to hide and watch.

They were creeping along the cliffs two-thirds of the way down, and Bob grinned with delight when he realised that they had missed the path he and Bob had found, and could not regain it.

He watched them go to and fro, trying to find a path that led upward, and from his position he could see one that seemed easy.

He hoped they wouldn't notice it, when suddenly it seemed to him that these Boers were strangely like his own friends, and that the one who was in command was surely Captain Deane.

He did not dare hail, for fear of alarming the enemy, and so he crept a little way down the path he had marked out, and waved a handkerchief.

They saw it after a little while, and, guided by his motioning arms, were directed up the path, now to the left round some projecting rock, and then back to the right for many yards, and then, perhaps, on hands and knees up a stiff incline.

"I thought you was Boers at first, sir," was his greeting to Captain Deane, when the latter came panting up to the top.

"You have helped us from an awkward position, my lad," said the skipper. "We had got too far down, and couldn't find a way back. 'Are all well?"

"Quite well, sir. I was going to Sir Peter from Master Bob, to say that if he sends forty men we can take the fort from the rear, while he has a go at 'em from the front."

"And now you can return with me. Sir Peter and I had the same idea, and I have all the men we can spare. Now lead us to where Master Bob is."

Bill led the way, which was comparatively easy, but the men were tired, and almost done up.

Before they could do anything, a rest and a mouthful of food was necessary, and so a halt was called.

Bob explained to Captain Deane the nature of the fort defences.

"I think we could rush the place, only before the men can get into position they'll see us. Still, if the enemy is kept busy in front, we may do it."

"I fancy, Bob, we had better send a note to Sir Peter, telling him how far he can rely on us. I think with you that at the first surprise we may get into the fort, but there are not enough of us to capture it. If we get in, it must be to give time to those in front to come up, and we must not start until they are within eight hundred yards of the place."

"That's so, Captain Deane. I think they'll be able to cover that distance while we are having a go at them, and once they come up, the fort will be ours."

"Very well, Bob. Send a note to Sir Peter. We will keep out of sight, and you can watch the battle, and give us the word when the right time comes. That is," he added, "if you are not too tired. You must be very weary, my dear lad."

"Not too tired to make sure of such a victory as we shall have," answered the lad, who then wrote the note, and sent it by Bill, post-haste for Sir Peter.

*   *   *   *

It was three o'clock in the morning, and Sir Peter and the men were finishing an early breakfast when Bill arrived with the letter.

To try and surprise the fort with so few men was too risky, Bob wrote, but when Sir Peter had got his men near enough, they would attack from the rear.

"Bob is getting cautious—a good sign," Sir Peter said, as he told Lieutenant Watkins the news.

"We are as ready as we were yesterday, Sir Peter, to attack in front. It must be the main attack that will win the day," said the young officer, pleased that after all his frontal attack was to come off. He had the old idea that pluck wins battles, and not bullets, and he knew that he had the bravest men under him that can be found anywhere, and was prepared to stake all on their courage.

But Sir Peter knew that bravery is not bullet-proof, and he therefore insisted on every available piece of cover being taken, and there was plenty.

The Boers—or some of them—were awake now, and were watching the British force in front, never suspecting that within three hundred yards, nicely hidden under the brow of the cliffs, another little army of Britons was lying in waiting.

The sailors came along in beautiful order, ten paces apart, stooping and seeking cover as soon as a few bullets from long range began to hit the ground near.

"There goes our beauty," cried one, and a shell came hurtling through the air from the four-point-seven gun, and, burying itself in the sand, did little harm.

"They don't know how to handle a gun," cried one sailor.

"Keep under cover, men," shouted Sir Peter, "and don't rush forward until you've picked out the next bit of shelter."

"Bill, I ain't been shaved for a month, and this is like coming to a barber's shop," cried one young sailor as a bullet scraped his cheekbone.

"You've got too much cheek, Ben, and the Boers is taking it down for you," was the laughing reply.

"Not them. I'll be a swell to-morrow about the face. Come on, Bill," and the two rushed forward a few paces, and then threw themselves down to escape the storm of bullets directed against them.

Here and there a man was hit, but so far the loss was extremely small, and Sir Peter was congratulating himself on it when a shell, possibly by chance, fell near a rock which sheltered four men.

Three were killed, and the fourth wounded, and the men, seeing this, began to clamour for a charge.

"It's better than being blown up by our own gun, and we not able to fire back," cried one.

"Silence, men! Have you forgotten your discipline?" called out the lieutenant.

"Trust him, he ain't. He'd give us discipline," whispered Ben to Bill, but silence prevailed, and nearer and nearer crept the line of attack.

Suddenly there was a shout from the fort.

"Fix bayonets—charge!" yelled the lieutenant, and in a moment, leaping over obstacles, racing with each other, mad with excitement, came the glorious British tars in an irregular line, converging on the fort.

From the rear, half of Captain Deane's men had reached the top of the cliff before being seen, and these poured a volley into the fort, and charged down, while the other men scrambled after them, leaving the boys to cover a possible retreat.

Bob was, however, with Captain Deane, and reserving his fire, he shot down a huge Boer who stood just behind the low wall of the rear of the fort taking aim at the invaders.

For a moment the defenders were borne back, then numbers prevailed, and they in turn were forced back, losing a man every moment.

Reinforced by the other men and some of the boys, who had disobeyed orders and joined in the attack, they held their own for a little, and then Captain Deane, Bob, and three men, found themselves in the midst of a circle of Boers, being thrust at and struck at from all sides.

A British cheer!

Some of the Boers turned to face Sir Peter's men as they came tumbling over the wall in front, others, falling on their knees, asked for quarter.

Bob threw his arms round one desperate fellow, who was about to smash in Captain Deane's head, while the sturdy skipper was engaged with another foe.

It was pandemonium for a moment, friend and foe were so mixed up that none dare fire; but the bayonets of the sailors were irresistible, and in less than five minutes the fort was theirs, and what were left of the Boers were prisoners.

"THERE WAS AN EXPLOSION, AND A HUGE MASS OF ICE FELL."

CHAPTER XXV.

WHEN Gilbert Romer found himself free, he started to reach the fort without delay, arriving there a few hours after its capture by Sir Peter and his gallant little army.

As soon as he had revived somewhat after his exhausting experiences, it was arranged that fifty of the most active of the men should accompany him, and should re-enter the caves by the way he had come out, while the others formally laid siege in front.

Bob and the boys were to go with him, the youngsters being good climbers; and Bob, delighted to see his uncle once again, was now keen for the rescue of the girls.

Most of the wounded men were doing well, the cold, pure air being beneficial to their wounds, Captain Ballance, despite his severe injuries, being out of danger already, and ready to chat with Sir Peter and Gilbert.

The dead were buried with honours, and as soon as the ceremony was over the spirits of the Jack Tars rose, and they were once more the merry, willing fellows who make light of all danger and trouble, and who are ready to prove that there is nothing that the British sailor will not dare.

All this time the "Nautilus" had been lying under water on top of the privateer, and Captain Deane, with a small party of his own men, decided at once to hurry back to her and to attempt the capture of the Boer vessel.

"Probably the enemy were not prepared for so long an immersion, and had not the air reservoirs filled, in which case they'll be half-dead," he explained.

"And if they show fight?" asked Sir Peter.

"I propose to board them, and capture the crew as they emerge."

"But, if they don't, they may try to escape."

"We will follow them until they do."

"Have you enough men?"

"Quite enough, Sir Peter; so, with your permission, we'll be off now."

Soon afterwards, Deane and a dozen men were marching back to the creek, and, putting on their diving-dresses, they entered the water.

The rope-ladder hung from the top of the "Nautilus," just as they had left it, and under their vessel lay the great hull of the privateer, as silent as though she were lifeless.

Buchan was delighted to see his comrades again, and reported all well. He had received plenty of fresh air from tubes pushed above water, and he had found the enemy obtaining air in the same way, and had promptly cut their pipes, since when they had not moved.

"I am afraid that they won't be quite so exhausted as I feared," Captain Deane said. "Still, we must try the experiment. We will now rise to the surface."

The vibration caused by the machinery and screws of the "Nautilus" must have been felt by those in the privateer, for no sooner had the British vessel risen than the other rose also.

In a moment Deane and his men had armed themselves and taken up a position on the deck of their own vessel, where they waited for the Boers to appear.

Presently the hatch of the privateer was gently raised a little, and Captain Deane ordered his men to the rear, where they would be safe from a sniper.

However, no Boer appeared, and Captain Deane hailed the vessel.

"Are you willing to surrender? Your comrades are our prisoners, and you can't escape," he called out.

"*You* can't, you verdomte rooinek," was the reply. "You'll never leave here."

And the privateer started to circle round, apparently with the idea of firing a torpedo from her bows.

The "Nautilus" circled, too, and in a minute the bows of the two vessels were pointing to the open sea.

This was evidently what the Boers had manœuvred for, as a second later the privateer fled full speed down the creek.

Captain Deane, blaming himself for allowing his opponent this opportunity for escape, sent the "Nautilus" after her, and in a short time the two vessels were in the open sea once more, the privateer heading for the opening in the ice through which they had come.

"She doesn't show fight this time," said Buchan. "Is she going to try and get away? She knows that we can catch her when we like."

"I can't think. They know that if they attempt to go through we shall smash them. We can't go in front to cut them off, or they will torpedo us; and they're not such fools as to believe we'll give them that chance."

"Can't we run against their screw and strip the blades?"

"We can always disable them like that; but I put that as a last resource. We want the vessel, and if she has no spare blades—and I saw none on shore—we should render her useless to us. No; we'll wait until we are close to the entrance, and see if they mean business, or whether this run is merely to try and shake us off."

The race continued, the "Nautilus" easily keeping close to the side of the privateer.

League after league they ploughed on together, seeming as careless of each other as consorts might be.

The distant mass of ice came nearer and nearer, and still the pace did not slacken.

They were half a mile away from the entrance when the privateer stopped.

"I thought it was bluff," said Buchan, grinning, as the "Nautilus" drifted alongside.

"Keep every man ready, Buchan," said Captain Deane. "She may turn on us at any moment, like she did before, in order to torpedo us."

"We are all ready, sir; but I think the Boers have had enough. They can't get away from us now, and they know it."

"Port, hard over! Full speed!" roared Deane, a moment after, and Buchan instinctively started the

engine, while the man at the steering-wheel turned it sharply round.

The two vessels grated together, and as they did so there was a splash at the bows of the privateer, and a torpedo could be seen speeding along the water.

"They're aiming at the entrance. They want to blow up the ice there, and block it so that none of us may ever escape," gasped Deane.

"The spiteful brutes," growled Buchan. "If they do, let's sink her."

"I moved their vessel, I think, Buchan, and spoilt their aim. But it will be a near thing. See, there it goes! Heavens! The current will take it right in."

"No, sir it's pointing twenty yards below."

And Buchan looked earnestly along a line of string he had stretched towards the entrance.

"Keep her going, Buchan. Don't let the villains have another quiet aim. You're wrong. The current has it; it will go right in and explode against the walls."

"No, sir; ten yards down. It's being carried towards the entrance, but it will strike before it gets the right direction. There!"

There was an explosion, and a huge mass of ice joined the heaving sea where the torpedo had exploded.

Then, when calm had come again, it was seen that the entrance was intact.

Once more the privateer leapt away, and tried to head for the entrance, but the circle was large, and after her sped the avenging "Nautilus."

Twenty yards divided them, and yard by yard the "Nautilus" crept up.

The privateer shot out another torpedo, and almost at the same moment the great steel nose of the "Nautilus" pressed into the stern of its opponent.

The blades of the screw struck it, and one by one were ripped off; and in one moment the privateer lay helpless.

The second torpedo hit the ice-wall fifty yards lower down, and again there was a tumbling of ice and the upheaval of water; and then all was quiet.

"We must tow our prize in, Buchan. She won't dare to sink now, and so half-a-dozen of the men must board her, and shoot if they open the hatch, unless they surrender and come up unarmed and singly."

"I'll send the men, sir," answered the engineer.

And soon the British sailors, angry when they learned how nearly they had been doomed to life captivity in these bleak regions, were in possession of the privateer's deck, and a hawser—made fast to her conning-tower—was fastened to the "Nautilus," so that the two were lashed together side by side.

"We don't go in front to receive a torpedo, Buchan," said Deane. "They'd sink us cheerfully, knowing that they'd be doomed at the same time."

"I believe they would, sir," said Buchan.

More slowly than they had come out, the two vessels returned to the creek, and after a vain attempt to break out, which led to a couple of Boers and one British sailor being wounded, the crew of the privateer surrendered, and Captain Deane took possession of the vessel that had done so much damage to the British Navy.

She was dirty, but luxuriously fitted, with fittings taken from her many prizes; but she lacked the scientific apparatus that had enabled those on board the "Nautilus" to see under the water.

But the terror of British shipping was helpless now; and, vexed as Captain Deane was at having to disable her, yet it was not without a feeling of satisfaction that he saw her inert and powerless.

CHAPTER XXVI.

MARGERY and 'Beth were not for long permitted to enjoy the privacy of their miserable cave.

As soon as Gilbert's flight was discovered, Van Leer visited them, half-mad with anger.

"So you helped him to escape?" he gasped, too angry to speak distinctly.

"It was my duty," was Margery's bold reply.

"You acknowledge it—you—you spy! You — you — enemy!" he roared. "If I thought I ever loved you, it was that I should own a rooinek wife who should be my slave. I thought how I would degrade you, you woman of the enemy. And now, come with me."

And, seizing her by the wrists, he dragged her from the cave into the public cave outside, in which were gathered the rest of the Boers.

'Beth followed, her bright little face glowing with indignation, ready to champion her sister at any cost.

"Are you men to permit this bully to hurt my sister?" she cried, as the Boers looked round, some with interest, some stolidly.

"I'll gag you," growled Van Leer. And then, turning to his comrades, he said: "This woman acknowledges to having helped the spy to escape. He will bring the rooineks upon you all."

A roar of anger burst from the bearded groups. Van Leer had made the affair personal to them.

"He is engaged to my sister. Your women would do as much for the men they love," shrilled 'Beth, placing herself in front, and quite regardless of danger.

"Our men are not spies. Those that help a spy and bring the enemy to kill us—what is it such a one deserves?" asked the Boer leader.

"Death!" was the chorussed cry, deep in tone, and so solemn that 'Beth turned pale, and Margery fell, limp and fainting, against the wall of the cave.

"You cowards! Do you murder women?" 'Beth cried, in an agony of despair.

"No, no!" some of the elder men answered, but the younger men shouted above them:

"Death! Death to all spies!"

"We will take a vote—a trial is unnecessary, for the woman has confessed. Hands up those who are for death!"

And the Boer leader looked round, and counted the many hands held up.

"Against!" he cried, and about a dozen were uplifted.

"You shall kill me first! You cowards—you great cowards!" cried 'Beth, placing her arms round her sister and facing the crowd, with her keen little face showing no trace of fear. Her attitude pleased the rough men there, and some shouted approval and others laughed.

"If I were a man I'd fight you all!" she cried, stamping her feet.

And again her defiance pleased them, so that some called to Van Leer to let the woman alone and see to the defences.

He glared at his comrades, but said nothing; and 'Beth, taking advantage of the momentary calm, half-carried, half-supported her sister back to the cavern.

But Van Leer had determined either to marry Margery or to have her killed, and he was a man of strong purpose.

As soon as he could leave his comrades unnoticed he crept quietly to the back of the far cavern.

He had an idea, and no longer demanded Margery's death.

He was exploring the back of the cave by the route which he was sure that Gilbert had taken, and his keen eye saw traces here and there, as he used his lantern, of his late prisoner's progress.

When he had found the path, he intended, while the other Boers were asleep, to fetch Margery, and to escape with her into the interior of the island, and leave his companions to fight as best they could.

Margery was sleeping fitfully in 'Beth's arms when, some hours later, he appeared.

Holding a pistol at 'Beth's head, he bade her and Margery rise and come with him.

If they made one sound, he whispered, he would shoot both; if they followed him quietly he would take them to the British camp, and leave them to plead for pardon for him.

If they were discovered escaping, he would be shot as well as they.

There seemed some reason for his action.

He was so base that it was easy to imagine him turning traitor and claiming a reward for restoring prisoners; and so the girls at once prepared to go with him, so eager were they to meet their friends again.

* * * *

The British, having placed the prisoners captured in the fort under proper guards, left for the burning mountain, Gilbert and Bob's special party going by the route that Gilbert had come, the others marching direct to where the Boers had already been located by scouts.

Van Leer and the two girls had reached the open mountain after great risk and much toil, when Gilbert and his little party were a little less than a mile away.

Bob saw the trio first, and drew his uncle's attention to them.

"It's Van Leer. He means mischief to the girls. We mustn't show ourselves," said Gilbert Romer, and he gave orders for all to keep under cover while he and Bob crept forward.

"Not that way, young lady," Van Leer said, as 'Beth turned south. "Your friends are this way."

"What, over the mountain?" the girl asked, suspicion showing itself in her face.

"Yes, that is the way," he answered.

"I don't believe it," she cried, boldly. "You said they were coming to attack your men, and so they must be coming from the sea."

"The sea is over there, too," he said.

"Margery, I feel sure he is deceiving us," 'Beth said. "From where we are we can see our friends whichever way they come, and we must wait here."

"You shall go with me, I say. You are a young fool. My men will catch you and shoot you," cried Van Leer, angrily.

"We can see them coming, too, and escape," said 'Beth, coolly. "Besides, my sister isn't strong enough to walk further without a rest. Mr. Romer is sure to bring aid, and if you mean to be our friend, I shall say all I can for you."

Van Leer drew his revolver and cocked it.

"You see this," he said, and the two girls recoiled. "Ah! you understand! You come with me, or I shall shoot Will you come?"

"Do you swear you will take us straight to our friends?" asked Margery.

He looked at her, so frail and pretty, and his eyes burned.

"I swear!" he answered.

Wearily the girls rose, and prepared to go on, when a shout of "'Beth!" "Margery!" made them turn quickly round to where Gilbert and Bob Romer stood, not a hundred yards away. The mountain was bare just there, and the two could conceal themselves no longer.

"Gilbert!" "Bob!" the girls answered, and turned to go to them.

Van Leer had replaced his revolver, but he pulled it out again, and was levelling it at Margery, when a slight crack was heard.

Bob had seen the action, and had fired at close quarters, and the Boer leader had fallen dead.

Margery ran to Gilbert and hid her face on his shoulder, too thankful for speech.

"Good shot, wasn't it?" Bob asked 'Beth, as he went up and shook hands as though they had just met after a short parting.

"It is dreadful—horrible! You've killed him!" she said, in awe stricken tones. "Oh, it is dreadful!"

"Just like a girl!" Bob grumbled. "You do her a good turn, and then she doesn't like it."

"Death is so terrible, Bob, that is all. But Margery and I are grateful indeed! You are so brave!"

"Oh, that's nothing!" Bob said, appeased at once, and trying hard to look modest.

Far below them they could see the British force approaching the caves,

spread out over a large portion of the country.

From the caves the Boers were already beginning to fire, and Gilbert, leaving the girls with a couple of men to protect them, led his following into the mountain over the path he had escaped by.

His appearance with some of his men from the rear of the cave a while later caused the Boers to surrender, the British casualties being very slight.

The island was now in the hands of Sir Peter and his friends, and soon the delighted girls were handed over to their father's care once more.

Arrangements were made for an early return to England, and as all could not possibly sail at once, about half of the British and all the Boers were left behind, to be fetched later, when the "Nautilus" would return with a spare screw for the privateer.

The return of the "Nautilus" to England was the greatest event in the memory of living man.

Her adventures were in every paper, and every man on board of her was interviewed.

Bob had his portrait published in fifty papers, and it was not his fault that he wasn't conceited.

Gilbert and Margery were married within a month of landing, and the wedding present they received from Sir Peter made them independent for life.

The millionaire adopted Bob as his son, and so his prospects are brighter still, and Bill Yeo has left the sea and is to act as Bob's valet.

Captain Deane received ten thousand pounds, and Buchan and all the crew were handsomely rewarded.

But what all value more than anything else are the thanks of Parliament extended to all who sailed in the "Nautilus" for their great services to British shipping, the extinction of which was threatened by the Boer Privateer.

THE END.